Seeking
Pack Redemption

Pack #3

Eve Langlais
New York Times Bestselling Author

Copyright © September 2011, Eve Langlais
Copyright © 2nd Edition April 2016
Cover art © Mina Carter, September 2011
2nd Edition Edits by Devin Govaere

Produced in Canada
Published by Eve Langlais
1606 Main Street, PO Box 151
Stittsville, Ontario, Canada, K2S1A3
http://www.EveLanglais.com

ISBN-13: 978 1988 328 27 0

ALL RIGHTS RESERVED

Seeking Pack Redemption is a work of fiction and the characters, events and dialogue found within the story are of the author's imagination and are not to be construed as real. Any resemblance to actual events or persons, either living or deceased, is completely coincidental.

No part of this book may be reproduced or shared in any form or by any means, electronic or mechanical, including but not limited to digital copying, file sharing, audio recording, email and printing without permission in writing from the author.

Prologue

He's going to kill her.

It killed Jaxon to see Bailey helpless in the monster's grasp. *My fault. All my fault. I should have fought harder. Been stronger. Not caved in to the wickedness controlling my mind.* A wickedness that haunted him still.

The nightmare of the past few days shamed him. He'd betrayed his pack, his brothers, but worse than all that, he had handed the woman he loved over to a killer and condemned her to torture. Harder to swallow, she'd forgiven him even though he deserved to die. *And if I don't do something, she'll perish right in front of me as I watch.*

Bunching his muscles, he strained to free himself, to move his frozen limbs, to no avail. He lacked the strength to fight the invisible chains that bound him, forcing him to stand as if a statue, a spectator to the unfolding events.

The disdain in his packmates' eyes shone clearly even from where they ranged across from him. Jaxon had earned their looks of disgust and rage. He'd have borne the same expression if he'd stood at their side and gazed upon someone who lacked the mental strength to fight Roderick's hold. Jaxon hated the rogue he'd unwillingly become. Yet . . . it still pulled the strings of his heart that they hated him because he loved them like brothers, and always would.

Handling the fact that his pack shunned him hurt, but he totally deserved it because what he'd done was unforgivable. He'd have gladly submitted to punishment if given the chance. But there was more than his need for atonement at stake here. He couldn't just sink into a ball of misery and pray to die. Nor could he remain kneeling, limbs frozen like a statue, and watch his mate suffer. *Not while I still breathe and live.*

However, the situation seemed untenable. The monster held Bailey by the throat. The claws tipping the vampire's fingers dug into her pale skin. To her credit, Bailey didn't whimper or cry. *She is so damned brave. I don't deserve her love.* How could he atone for his actions? How could he save her?

Jaxon bided his time and waited for his moment, that single, momentary lapse of attention when the leash the twisted creature held over his will would slip, loosen enough for him to strike.

The bloodsucking entity who had once been one of them, a Lycan and leader of his pack, laughed—a chilling sound meant for his brothers who faced off against him.

"So nice of you to join us," the vampire hissed.

"Let her go, Roderick. There is no escape," Gavin yelled having shifted into his human shape.

Jaxon could see the strain in his ex-friend's body as Gavin tried to hide his fear, a fear not for himself but the woman being held victim.

"Look, my incubator," Roderick said in a low, mocking tone to Bailey. "Your dogs have arrived and are already barking orders. Shall I take them as I've taken your other lover?"

Jaxon's head hung as the monster mocked his inability to fight his mental grasp. *Just give me a chance. A chance to save her.* A prayer he hoped didn't go unheeded. He'd love to shove the vampire's head into a place the sun didn't shine. Actually, on second thought, he'd prefer to shove it in the sun where the monster would hopefully die.

"No. Leave them alone," Bailey cried. Her brave reply caused the vampire to tighten his grip, puncturing her flesh until rivulets of red ran down her skin. The coppery scent of her blood roused Jaxon's beast where it paced inside his mind. *It harms our mate.* Growling, his inner wolf demanded action and tested the bounds of their mental captivity. *Soon,* Jaxon promised. *Watch. Wait.* He needed to wait for the right moment.

"I'm going to kill you," Wyatt shouted, forgoing his beast shape to speak. Jaxon ignored the glare flicked his way that screamed, "Dead man." It wouldn't be the first time Jaxon had drawn Wyatt's ire. *But this time I totally deserve it.*

Roderick laughed, a grating sound that

conjured images of dark dungeons replete with misery and pain. "I've faced death before, numerous times, I might add. Apparently, that lord of darkness has no use for me because I'm still here. And keep in mind, if you try anything, the first to go will be your precious mate."

Head bowed, gaze averted, Jaxon could nevertheless guess that Roderick tightened his grip because Bailey struggled to breathe. Choking sounds escaped her as her legs thrashed in panic. Oh, how his inability to act burned.

"Bastard." Gavin whispered the word, but everyone heard it. The benefit of being a Lycan included enhanced hearing, among other things, a curse for those who sought privacy.

"Is that any way to speak to your master?" Roderick replied. "Kneel for me, dogs. Bow to me, and maybe I'll let you live and serve."

"Never," Wyatt vowed.

"Funny, your friend here once said that. Shall I show you how I taught him to serve his master?"

Bracing himself, Jaxon waited for the tenebrous touch of evil to invade his mind. The pervasive and unbreakable mind control that fucked him over so royally and made him dance like a marionette. Except . . . The crushing pain never arrived. As a matter of fact, the pressure in his head eased, and his wolf growled. *Now?*

His brothers must have fought a mental invasion and won because the unnatural one screamed, "Kill them. Kill them all!"

"No." The word emerged as the smallest of whispers, but Jaxon still forced it past numb lips, including a lower lip that tingled from the bite Bailey had given them in the mating exchange. This reminder of her faith and love gave him strength. *I will not watch my friends and mate die.*

Pushing with all his strength against the paralysis in his limbs, Jaxon sprang up from his crouch and half shifted. The bones in his face and hands reshaped themselves, a familiar agony he could ignore. Hair sprouted in tufts while his fingers grew claws. Strength flowed through him.

It didn't go unnoticed. "Down, dog!" Roderick bellowed.

The crushing weight and torturous needles of Roderick's attack slammed against the walls of his mind. *Holy fuck* did it hurt, but Jaxon kept moving, his mouth opening and releasing a mournful howl, the only weakness he'd allow himself.

Despite the pain and the command to heel, Jaxon sank his teeth into the vampire's arm. Blood spurted, and he inadvertently tasted it. Foul and putrid, the taste caused his stomach to roil, but he didn't relent. He clenched harder, swallowing the unnatural essence that flooded his mouth, not daring to gag or spit lest he lose his grip.

The hand holding Bailey went slack, which released her. She slumped to the ground as Jaxon grappled with Roderick, the blood he'd swallowed burning its way down, churning his stomach as fire shot through his veins. *Dammit, I think he's poisoned me.* Not that he truly cared at the moment, not when he still held the vampire in fingers tipped with claws. Around him he could hear the sounds of battle as his packmates engaged Roderick's army of rogue wolves. If he could just hold Roderick off long enough for them to fight their way through, then maybe Bailey could escape this fucking mess.

Jaxon snapped his sharp teeth at Roderick's face and almost smiled when the creature recoiled.

Despite Jaxon's minor victory, the vampire remained strong, and worse, Jaxon not only fought his opponent's body but the attacks on his mind as well. The invisible needles struck, burning, ripping, torturing his psyche, but still Jaxon tried, oh how he tried, to rip out the bastard's throat. Tried to hurt him, kill him, end the vampire's monstrous existence. But despite Jaxon's wolfman shape and strength, Roderick still proved more powerful, and Jaxon knew he wouldn't be able to keep him at bay forever. *And when I let go, there's nothing stopping him from going after Bailey and my friends. I can't allow it.*

The creeping tentacles of Roderick's power began to seep in to try to control him, and Jaxon lost his hold on his half-shift as he fought back. Back in his human form again, Jaxon had only a heartbeat to decide his next step. There was only one real option.

A glance to the side showed Bailey, crouched on the ground, her eyes wide with fright. *I can't let Roderick have her.* Tears in his eyes, he yelled, "I love you, Bailey. Tell them all I'm sorry." With his final words spoken, he surged forward against the vampire.

Someone deciphered his intent and hands grasped for him. Fabric ripped free as momentum toppled Jaxon and Roderick over the edge of the precipice where they stood.

As they both plunged, tumbling head over heels in the air, Jaxon heard Bailey scream and sob harshly, sounds that signaled she lived. All that mattered really.

Jaxon smiled as he plummeted. *She's safe.* He used that serene, two-word chant to keep his lips sealed when he hit the first rock. And the second. . . .

By the time he hit the rapidly moving water, he was praying for death.

Chapter One

Months later...

The craving for chocolate hit her hard. Ooey, gooey, melt-in-her-mouth goodness. Rubbing her rounded belly, Thea rose from the couch and headed to the kitchen, but just like poor Old Mother Hubbard's, her cupboards were bare. The silly children's rhyme made her smile as she perused the shelves. Saltine crackers, cans of soup, some stale cereal. No chocolate. *I guess I should have done some grocery shopping before coming home from work.*

A rumble, loud in the closed-in kitchen, made her gasp then giggle. "Aren't you the demanding one?" she said with a smile in the direction of her midsection. "Your daddy still isn't home from work, though. I guess we'll have to wait and hope he's willing to go back out and get us a treat." Another grumble answered her. "I know. I know. I want some chocolate, too."

She glanced at the kitchen clock on the wall. Eight thirty-seven. Still early enough that a walk up the street to the corner store wasn't unfeasible. David probably wouldn't like it; her neighborhood wasn't exactly known for its quality inhabitants, but then again, her live-in boyfriend of almost three months wasn't here.

Given his recent work schedule, who knew when he'd arrive?

I'm hungry and a grown woman. I can go to the store if I want to. Brave words, now why did she feel like a naughty child about to do something bad?

After grabbing her coat and slipping on her shoes, she patted her pocket to check for her wallet before letting herself out of the apartment and locking the door. She'd be gone only a few minutes. Heck, she'd probably make it there and back, plus eat the treat, before David deigned to show. Or so she hoped. Given the frequency with which David's temper flared lately, she didn't want to do anything to set him off.

As she walked the two short blocks to the store, she couldn't help thinking on her boyfriend. He'd seemed so perfect when they first met. Working as a cashier at the local Walmart, she couldn't help but notice him when he showed up with a cartful of junk food. The attraction was instantaneous. Then again, only someone lacking a pulse would have not reacted to his striking good looks: just shy of six foot with a lanky build, tousled blond hair, and puppy-brown eyes. His shy smiles just made him cuter.

Every day after that, he showed up without fail, patiently waiting in her line even if other cashiers tried to wave him over. It took him four shopping trips before he mustered the courage to ask her out. Her yes emerged embarrassingly quickly. They went on one date—dinner and a movie—before she fell into bed with him. It wasn't like she was a slut. She'd only ever been with a few guys before David, and only after dating a few weeks first, but something about him, she couldn't pinpoint what, drew her. Made her forget her usual rules about waiting for sex, and the next thing she knew she was naked on the sheets of her bed as he thrust into her. Overcome with lust for her, which she'd found totally endearing at the time, he'd even bitten her during the act, something he apologized for after.

After that night, they became virtually inseparable, more because he couldn't stand to be away from her. He more or less moved in with her right away, only leaving her when they went their separate ways for work. Despite the speed of their courtship—and her misgivings—that first month was glorious. Then something changed. No, something didn't change. Someone changed, and it was him.

The man with the sweet smiles turned broody, and he watched her constantly, his eyes almost feverish and possessed of something dark. If she didn't know better, she would have said evil lurked in those depths. Foolishness of course. Harder to ignore were the changes in his personality. Changes that made her face reality.

"I don't think this is working out," she mustered the courage to say when he got home from work in a foul temper.

In the process of firing her shoes across the apartment, because he didn't like that she'd left them at the door, he froze.

"What are you trying to say?" he replied, keeping his back to her.

Taking a deep breath, she found the courage to tell him the words she'd practiced for the last week in her head. "I'm saying that perhaps we should have dated longer and not moved in so quickly. I think we need a break." In other words, he needed to leave because she couldn't handle his mood swings anymore.

His shoulders stiffened, and she braced herself for a verbal flaying. One hand on the phone, she was ready to dial 911 if it went further than words. The face he turned to her would have put a begging puppy to shame.

"Thea." He whispered her name brokenly. "You're right; I should go. I'm wrong for you. So wrong." Tears filled his eyes, and she tried to stay strong, tried to hold on to her resolve . . .

He dropped to his knees and buried his face against her legs, hugging them loosely, the picture of dejection. "I'm so sorry I've been such a bastard. The things I have to do when I leave here . . ." He didn't expand, going silent like he always did when she asked about his job. "It's like I have two people inside me. The man who loves you and would do anything to make you smile and the bastard who is frustrated and needs to vent."

"I understand your job is stressing you out, but you can't treat me like that, David. I won't allow it."

His grip on her tightened, and a frisson of fear made her wonder if she should have tempered her words. The hold on her relaxed.

"*You're right. So right. And I've been such a dog. But I promise to do better.*" *He raised moist eyes rimmed in red.* "*Give me a chance, Thea. Please. You have to. I'll die without you. I can't lose you. I-I love you.*"

And she loved him, too, didn't she? Besides, was she really the type of woman to call it quits because her boyfriend was a little stressed out because of work? He loved her. Didn't he deserve a second chance? Was she ready to go back to being alone?

Despite a little voice that told her to stay strong, she forgave him, and they made love. Things were good for a few weeks, then his jerk side came back, but she ended up looking past this less-than-pleasant aspect of his personality because, despite the fact that they had used condoms, the unthinkable happened. She ended up pregnant.

To her surprise, David was ecstatic, and for a short while, things were good again. He smiled and laughed a lot, and if at times she found him eyeing her oddly or he made love to her roughly, with none of the previous attention to her pleasure, then she downplayed it. Blamed it on the stress of his work. Blamed it on the fact that they struggled to make ends meet. In other words, she made excuses for his behavior.

But those excuses sounded false even to her.

I should have thrown his ass out when I had the chance because if it weren't for the baby, I'd park his stuff on the curb and change my locks. The very thought seemed traitorous. How could she even think that? They'd created life together. So, despite his mood swings and her uncertain feelings, with a baby on the way, she owed it to the child to attempt to make things work. *Whether I like it or not.*

When she arrived at the corner store, she ended up buying several chocolate bars: Oh Henry!, Mars, 3 Musketeers. Oh, and a few packages of Reese's Pieces. She also picked up some plain chips with an onion dip in case her craving suddenly shifted. Purchases paid for, she hurriedly walked back to her apartment, a sudden worry making her wish she'd not chosen to go out after dark. She watched every shadow, skirted every alley entrance until she reached the safety of her building. About to insert the key in the lock for her apartment, she stifled a scream when the door was abruptly flung open. David stood in the entrance and glared at her.

"Where the fuck were you?" he snapped.

Lovely. Angry-at-the-world David was home. *I should have eaten the crackers.* She held up her bags and attempted to calm him, reminding herself that his ire stemmed from his worry over her. "I was hungry, so I went to buy some stuff. I was only gone a few minutes."

"I was only gone a few minutes," he mimicked in a high-pitched voice. "Do you know what I thought when I got here and you were gone?"

Blinking, she tried to actually figure out where his extreme anger came from. Did he fear she'd get mugged and killed over chocolate and chips? "I'm sorry. I didn't think it was a big deal. Next time I'll leave a note." Because she refused to ask for permission to go out on her own.

"There won't be a next time," he snarled. "From now on, you don't leave this apartment unless I'm with you."

"Excuse me? Don't you think that's a little extreme? I just went two blocks to get a snack. It's not a big deal. I didn't even see anybody on my way there and back."

"You wouldn't see them coming. My enemies know how to hide their presence from someone blind and deaf like you. Humans are so easy to fool."

The tone of his rant made the hairs on her head tingle. What the hell was he talking about? "Have you been drinking? Because you're not making any sense." She moved to go around him, only to squeak as he grabbed her and slammed her up against the wall.

"Don't you mock me." His voice emerged low and menacing. It went well with the scary light in his eyes, which she could have sworn held a reddish hue. "I've allowed you freedom because I didn't want to jeopardize the baby, but if you're going to take foolish risks, then you leave me no choice. You will obey me or face the consequences."

"Let go of me. You're scaring me."

He shook her instead, each shake slamming her back into the wall. "You should be scared. You have no idea what you're dealing with. But you will. Soon." A laugh left his lips, a chilling sound she didn't recognize at all and that made her blood run cold.

Who was this stranger before her? He looked like David, smelled like David, but the David she knew would never have talked to her like this. Never threatened or manhandled her in this way.

"What's wrong with you?" she cried. "Why are you acting like this? I thought you loved me." Did he suspect she didn't feel the same way? That she wanted him gone?

"I'd love to hear you scream," he chortled in a tone she didn't recognize.

Stunned disbelief held her tongue as the face before her contorted, the muscles moving in ways that shouldn't have been possible. They morphed for a second, a single blink of time, into an almost canine expression. Then David's face returned, the expression soft and haunted. The grip on her arms loosened.

"Run," he whispered. "I can't hold him off for long. Run, Thea. Run as far and fast as you can. Find my brother, Trent. He'll be strong enough, I hope, to protect you."

"What are you saying? Brother? What brother? And why do you want me to leave?"

He groaned and shook his head, his eyes

closing as if pained. "Please, Thea. I can't get him out of my mind. I can't stop him from hurting you. Please. You need to go."

She didn't move. How could she with the father of her child so obviously conflicted? He needed a doctor and some meds because it was becoming obvious he suffered from some kind of mental malady. "I'm not leaving you when it's obvious you need help. We'll get through this together. You can fight this thing, David." She reached up to touch his face. He flinched.

A tremor shook him, and he grunted as he reeled away from her. "No, Thea, You don't understand. Leave. Now!"

The conflict on his face, so visible as his muscles shifted under his skin, as if he fought some inner battle, almost rooted her feet. It was the red flare of his eyes and the sense of something cold entering the room, a slimy feel of *evil*, that shocked her into realizing there was something deeply wrong with David. Something more than perhaps drugs could counter.

She backed away as he hunched over, his breaths coming fast and hard. Her chilly sensation deepened. She placed her hand on the door, about to turn the knob when he spoke. The mocking voice that emerged wasn't the man she knew.

"Where do you think you're going, my breeding bitch?"

Flinging the door open, she forwent a reply

and instead ran up the hall, heading for the elevator. She didn't make it. Rough hands gripped her from behind and slammed her against the wall. A short scream left her as the stranger in David's body leered at her. If she didn't know better, she'd wager a demon possessed him. Eyes glowing a hellish red, he leaned into her, inhaling deeply before licking her—a long, wet swipe of his tongue that made her shudder.

"Stop it. Let go of me!"

"I don't think so. No more Mr. Nice Guy for you. Time to cut short the game and bring you to your new home."

As she struggled against the iron grip pinning her to the wall, she spat, "I don't know who and what you are, but I'm not going anywhere with you. Help!" She shouted as loud as she could. "Help me! Someone call the pol—"

He slapped a hand over her mouth, too late. A door opened a few feet away, and a head popped out.

"Hey, buddy," the bald stranger said as he stepped into the hall. He began to frown. "I think you need to let the lady go."

"Mind your fucking business," snarled her possessed boyfriend.

"I don't think so," the Samaritan replied, cracking his knuckles in a menacing fashion.

The violent entity let her go and turned to fully face her neighbor. She inched away, her eyes not leaving them as they squared off.

"Humans," scoffed the stranger in her boyfriend's body. "So mouthy, and yet so fragile."

A cry left her lips as, quicker than her mind could comprehend, David reached out and twisted the other guy's head. A sharp crack and the man who tried to step in stared at nothing. The monster in the hall dropped the limp body and turned to face her.

"Going somewhere?"

"Fuck. Oh fuck. Oh fuck." She couldn't stop repeating the foul words over and over, nothing else strong enough to express her extreme horror at the situation. She stumbled backward, not wanting to look away from the creature stalking her with a red glint in its eyes. It only prolonged the inevitable.

With an almost gleeful, "Come to papa," he pounced.

After a brief struggle—no real contest against his strength—a fist met her face once, twice, before she passed out.

As it turned out, unconsciousness beat reality, or so she discovered when she woke up chained in a cell.

I should have run.

Chapter Two

God, what an idiot. He was almost as stupid as his missing younger brother. Walked right into the trap and pretty much handed himself to the assholes lying in wait. Worse, Trent knew his two buddies would come sniffing after him when he didn't meet them at the rendezvous point, which meant he'd soon have company—along with the teasing that came along with it. He could hear it now: *"Caught like a wet-behind-the-ears pup."*

Goddamned hillbillies! What else to call the gap-toothed idiot who owned enough brains to shoot him with silver buckshot—enough to incapacitate his wolf—but not enough intelligence to kill him? *Stupid, because once I get loose, I'm going to rip his fucking head off.* Adding insult to injury, a second inbred asshole had tranquilized him with a dart. It almost made a wolf wonder what the hell they intended. He might even ask before he tore their throats out. Although humans were generally considered off-limits, in some cases, such as this one, where they knew more than they should, there was only one solution available.

First, though, he needed to get free. Whoever his captor's father was, which in this fucked-up part of the mountains could even be his grandpa or uncle, he'd taught the boy how to tie knots well. But he'd forgotten to tell him that Lycans, short of being bound in silver chains, couldn't be held by conventional means for long. When straining didn't work, Trent coaxed his wolf forth, and the violence of the change, which contorted his body and ripped his clothes to shreds, snapped the rope.

On four paws, he hit the floor and sniffed. Bad idea. According to the malodorous scents hitting his snout, this place had never encountered the cleansing touch of a mop, broom, or anything resembling a cleaner. He did, however, catch the rancid stench of his captors. Now he just had to find the buck-toothed idiot and his equally stupid sidekick and teach them why it was a bad idea to shoot a Lycan in the ass with silver.

Not wanting to change back into his human shape to open the door, Trent dove through the filth-encrusted window. Already half covered in cardboard, it gave easily against his weight, with the remaining shards of glass tinkling to the ground. He shook his thick coat, which sent the lingering bits flying. The sharp pricks of broken glass, trying to bite through his callused paws, didn't really bother him, but he still stepped gingerly out of the mess until he got clear. Running on wounded feet was never a pleasant experience.

Raising his head, he sniffed. Ah, the cool,

crisp scent of the forest. How he loved it. He just wished he'd come here for a better reason.

His little brother David was missing. Had been for about six months now. But had David's pack leader told Trent right away?

Nope. The bastard hid it from him. And yet he couldn't fault David's alpha. His brother had told his alpha he was going back home to Trent's small pack. Then David turned around and for some fucked-up reason never Trent during their weekly phone calls that he'd left. Why lie?

And what really happened? Trent only began to suspect something wrong when calls to his brother's cell started going unanswered, and then the phone became disconnected. Concerned, he called his brother's pack alpha. Talk about a sucker-punch to the gut finding out David hadn't been seen or heard from since he'd left months and months before.

It made no sense. His brother wasn't the lone-wolf type, so where had he gone? *And why did the little prick lie to me?*

Given how long it had been since anyone last saw him, Trent was more worried than he liked to admit, especially since an order from the Pack Council had come down the line saying there was danger out there. Something stalked their kind. Or, as the whispers claimed, "The bogeyman's coming to get us."

The smaller Lycan groups were ordered to merge with the larger packs in gated compounds.

Curfews were set. People, Lycans like himself, who usually feared nothing, were told to not leave unless in large groups and to never exit the safety of the compounds after dark. Hell, even dusk was off-limits.

Rumors abounded about the strange decree, rumors aided by the disappearances of wolves, mostly male ones. Large packs of rogues kept cropping up and breaking the rules—mainly causing trouble and violence among the humans. Those rogues didn't live for long once found. The packs had enforcer groups set up especially to deal with them. Trent even joined a few for the thrill of the hunt. Everyone needed to do their part to ensure the out-of-control wolves didn't draw the wrong kind of attention—a.k.a. human—to their kind.

While Trent enjoyed the dynamics of a group bent on keeping their secret safe through violence—something he excelled at—he didn't like the order forcing him both to leave his home in the woods and to unite his small group of Lycans with an adjoining group. He didn't like it but couldn't deny something was wrong, and whatever it was, it was coming after his people. The safety of the families under his care mattered more than his pride.

As an alpha himself, Trent knew that living under another's rule sucked, even if he had nothing but the greatest respect for Nathan, one of the council leaders, despite his youth. But no martial law, or logic, could stop Trent from leaving to look for his brother when he discovered him missing, although his temporary alpha had tried.

Nathan sat behind his desk while Trent paced across from him, instinct warning him he wasn't going to like what the council leader had to say.

"I've had people looking into your brother's disappearance."

"And?"

"By all indications, he's gone rogue."

"Bullshit," Trent declared. "David doesn't have the backbone to become a lone wolf."

"Who says he is? We think he's joined up with a group of rogues."

Trent couldn't help his scoffing tone. "I don't believe it. My brother wouldn't harm a fly. He's not capable of it."

Nathan sighed noisily. "What I'm going to tell you is classified, although you've probably heard rumors. The rogues aren't acting independently. Hell, they're not joining these rebel groups because they want to. Someone is forcing them to act in ways contrary to their beliefs and our laws."

"So, what, there's an alpha out there threatening them to obey?"

"Not threatening. Our enemy is using mind control to fuck with them."

A snort escaped him. "Don't tell me you believe that! I've heard that ridiculous rumor. A vampire supposedly controlling wolves. What a load of crap."

"It's the truth."

"Really? Then why haven't we had a meeting about it? Why haven't you gone public with the knowledge?"

The alpha drummed his fingers on his desk.

Trent smirked. "Because it's not true."

"Oh, it's true all right, but can you imagine announcing it to the pack at large? Controlling them is hard enough as it is, even with the Pack Laws. How do you think they'd react if they knew vampires existed and that one in particular can control their minds and make them dance to his tune like marionettes?"

"I think they'd demote your ass as pack leader and council member and lock you up in a padded room," Trent retorted. "I don't know what game you and the council are playing, but I'm not falling for this falsehood. I'm leaving to find my brother, martial law or not."

"It's dangerous out there. You'll make a perfect target for the creature seeking to strengthen his ranks."

"I'll take my chances."

"Leave, and you'll be declared rogue," Nathan growled. "And be warned. Once you step out of those gates, there's no coming back."

"Then so be it."

Family was more important to Trent than the pack. David, despite his many faults, was all Trent had left.

Although Nathan didn't come out and publicly declare him rogue as Trent prepared to leave, he did have a warning posted that any who left, other than during designated supply runs, could not return to the pack. Once Trent walked through those gates, there was no turning back.

Trent waved as he drove by. And he didn't leave alone. His two best friends, Marc and Darren, came with him, refusing to be left behind, stating, "Like hell are we letting you have all the fun and scars," because, as Marc added, "Chicks dig scars." Of course, their kind didn't scar easily, with silver and the mating bite about the only things that could permanently mark them, but that didn't dissuade his best buds. God, he loved the stupid bastards. In many respects, they were closer to him than his own brother.

It took them almost two months to track David, following his path from the pack he'd left to a small town in the middle of nowhere, which they'd almost bypassed except that their lunch stop at a fish-and-chips stand saw his tempura-covered halibut wrapped in a bit of newspaper. Wolfing down his lunch until only the wrapper remained, he almost spat out his last mouthful. In the picture staring up at him, grainy and grease-stained, was his brother, his arm around a girl. Ketchup covered the article, which made him snarl in frustration. It took only a little digging to find the story, and what he read in the dilapidated motel room that he'd rented chilled him to the bone.

WOMAN MISSING AFTER BOYFRIEND KILLS NEIGHBOR!

Local resident Thea Papadopoulos was last heard screaming in the hall of her apartment building moments before her live-in boyfriend, David Emerson, killed a neighbor who stepped in to offer aid. An eyewitness, watching through the peephole in their door, described the murder as chilling, saying, "He just wrung his neck like it was a chicken." Authorities have yet to nab the killer or to recover his girlfriend, who was last seen by a pedestrian walking their dog as Emerson carried her limp body out to his car. The vehicle has since been recovered in the parking lot adjoining the national park, but despite teams of searches, including canine units, they've yet to recover either of them. The investigation is ongoing.

Punching a hole in the motel wall didn't change the content of the article. And yelling didn't bring his brother back with answers. *Because I don't believe it.* Disbelief, though, wouldn't return his brother. At least Trent had a place to begin his search, even if he feared what he'd find at the end of that path. The article had been written six weeks ago, so picking up any trail would prove challenging, but not impossible for someone of his ilk.

The town didn't have an active pack, the local group having moved on because of the mandate from the Lycan council. Not that Trent needed their help. When he found his brother, and he would, he'd kick his ass himself and find out the truth because the David he knew wouldn't hurt a human. Heck, his little brother didn't even like the fact that his wolf hunted squirrels.

So what would make his little brother snap? Could it be the girl he apparently lived with? A girl he'd kept secret? Was he on drugs? Maybe the witness had been mistaken and the guy just looked like David. A ton of questions and no answers. Yet.

Equipped with a knapsack and walkie-talkies, he and his friends parked in the same lot where David's car had been found. All around them the forest loomed, a national park with hundreds of acres of untouched woods, a favorite hunting ground, he'd bet, for wolves who needed to stretch their four legs. And a great spot for inbred, country hicks to prey on unsuspecting victims.

For the moment, forget his brother, Trent's rogue status with the pack, and even his reason for being there. First things first. He had some fucking hillbillies to track because, while David was the nice one in the family, Trent wasn't. He'd gotten some of his dad's old-school attitude, his favorite one being an eye for an eye. Or, in this case, a total ass whooping, his favorite kind.

With night falling quickly this time of the year, autumn's grip clear in the changing color of the leaves, he wondered if he'd be better off waiting for the hicks to return to their cabin. *But I do so enjoy a good hunt.*

About to enter the woods in pursuit of his quarry, he halted as the forest around him turned abruptly silent. The air grew heavy and pressed on him, and the hair on his back stiffened and stood on end. Danger approached. A cautious sniff made his snout wrinkle as the crisp scent of the woods was overlain with something unpleasant, almost a putrid scent but mixed with something familiar, a hint of wolf, but a wolf like nothing he'd scented before.

What the fuck?

Something clutched at him, not physically but scrabbled against his head, trying to invade his mind. He whipped his head from side to side in an attempt to shake the feeling. He growled, frustrated when he still couldn't find something to attack. The pressure on his brain increased, and his hackles rose higher as his low rumble deepened.

The probing of his mind abruptly disappeared. Before he could wonder about it, he heard the crack of a gunshot, followed by two more. Immediately, he sprang into motion and barreled into the trees to follow the direction of the shot, which, not surprisingly, seemed to coincide with the increasing strength of the vile scent.

He stumbled into a clearing and halted as a man with vivid green eyes and a tight-lipped expression whirled and aimed his gun at him.

"I see Roderick has new recruits," he said with a mirthless laugh. "Not for long."

Trent rolled before the stranger finished pulling the trigger. The blast hit the dirt beside him. Trent kept moving as the gunman kept firing, only his speed and reflexes saving him from all but a light scoring along his side. A rustle in the brush saw his assailant whirling to fire as a pair of huge shapes leapt from the shadows, with Marc and Darren finally making an appearance. They tackled the stranger, who seemed not at all perturbed he had to fight off wolves. Even more fucked up, he almost got the upper hand until Marc got his teeth around the stranger's neck.

Before Marc could tear it out, Trent quickly changed shape to say, "Don't kill him. We need to question him."

Pinned under their combined weight, his neck in a deadly vise, the green-eyed shooter laughed. "I've got nothing to tell you, rogue."

"You know what we are?" Trent sniffed but couldn't decipher the stranger's odor from the heavy hunter's perfume he wore, some kind of bottled animal piss.

"I'd say the fact I didn't scream like a little girl when you shifted answers that question."

"Why did you try to shoot me?"

"I shoot all rogues." The answer emerged flat, despite the green sparks of hatred in his eyes.

"And what makes you so sure I'm a rogue? I'm sure other wolves use these woods, and it's not like rogues wear a sign."

"Are you denying your status?"

"Nope. But I still want to know why you're going around shooting my kind. Whether I've chosen to leave the pack or not doesn't mean I'm going to let some fucking human kill Lycans."

"Human?" The stranger laughed. "That's funny. As for shooting on sight, the pack is gone from this area. And what remains are rogues, pure and simple. I've made it my mission to kill those serving Roderick. The less minions he has, the better. I only live to see him dead."

Moving meant he stood closer to their captive. Trent's lip curled before he knelt. "I don't give a fuck who this Roderick is or what your beef with him is. I'm no one's minion. I went rogue to search for my brother, David. Looks like me but smaller and younger. Have you seen him around?"

"I haven't seen him." The vivid green eyes assessed him, and Trent returned the favor. While not dark-skinned, the man on the ground was an ethnic mix with light cocoa skin and curly hair. Unshaven and wearing clothes that had seen much better days, he looked haggard except for the bright light in his eyes. This was a man on a mission.

Trent leaned lower and sniffed to confirm his suspicions. A wolf under all that strong scent, a wolf whose demeanor indicated he had nothing left to lose. It made him dangerous.

"He's wolf," he announced. "And a rogue just like us, I'll bet."

"Correct."

"Explain again why you're hunting our kind?" Trent asked. A niggling sense told him that the answer to David's disappearance lay in the strange wolf's words.

"I exterminate rogues. Those who've let themselves get taken by Roderick, although my ultimate target is the vampire himself."

"Vampire?"

"You heard me. Guy who sucks blood, sleeps in the day, and can control those weaker than himself with his mind."

Trent snorted. "Don't tell me you're one of those idiots who believes those rumors."

"Not rumors. Truth."

Releasing their captive's neck, his friends shifted back, curiosity bright in their eyes.

"How do you know?" Darren asked. "Have you seen this supposed vampire?"

The other man nodded. A heavy sigh left him. "Roderick used to be my alpha and Nathan's father. You've heard or met Nathan, I assume?" At their nods, he continued. "When Roderick was sentenced to death for crimes against the pack, the council instead brokered a deal with the vampires. And before you say anything, my packmates and I had a hard time believing it, too, until we met Roderick. The vamps turned Roderick into one of them."

Trent held up his hand. "Wait a second, you want me to believe Nathan's dad is some kind of vampire? His dad is dead. Executed, from what I know, for crimes against the pack. And when I told Nathan I was leaving, he never told me to look out for his dad, although he did try to feed me some crazy bullshit about a bloodsucker who could control minds. Is his delusion contagious?"

"Roderick didn't die, at least not in a conventional sense. But from what you're saying, the pack has finally revealed the truth about Roderick and what he can do. About time. I know Nathan was trying to keep it quiet for fear of causing panic or even scoffing, which would lead to people not taking the safety advice seriously."

"Nathan and the council haven't said jack shit," Trent offered. "He told me this in private. All the packs know is the bullshit story he and the other council members have been feeding us about how we're being stalked and need to stick close together until the danger is caught."

"Forget catch. We need to kill the fucker. If only he'd sit still long enough for me to kill him. I don't know how many times I've shot Roderick. The bastard just won't fucking die."

Trent rose. "I've heard enough. He's obviously gone mad and is of no help to us."

"What are we going to do about him?"

Darren asked.

Trent eyed the stranger, who lay placidly on his back, hands laced under his head, and wore an expression of fake calm. But Trent could see the nerve ticking in his jaw.

Could he really kill the man for believing in fairy tales, a tale even an alpha was touting as truth? "Who are you?"

"Jaxon."

Darren frowned. "That name is familiar. I think I heard some of that new pack we were with talking about him. Something about him betraying them."

"Is that true?"

Guilt and sadness flooded Jaxon's face. "Unfortunately. Roderick caught me when we were bringing Bailey, a victim of his, back to the pack. I didn't know he'd left a ticking time bomb in my mind until I woke up in his dungeon with the realization that I'd handed the woman I loved to a monster."

"You gave him your mate?" Marc couldn't stem his incredulity.

Jaxon nodded his head. "It seemed Bailey was a dormant Lycan, but she didn't know it. Didn't know anything about our kind. When my pack brothers and I met her, she immediately called to our wolves. They marked and claimed her. But before my turn arrived, she got pregnant. For some reason, that knowledge triggered a compulsion Roderick left in my head and I ended up kidnapping her and bringing her to the vampire."

"Wow, aren't you a fucking prize, handing her over to someone else. No wonder the pack shunned you."

"I say we kill him," Darren growled. "The pack doesn't like those who betray."

Trent shook his head. "And what makes him any different than us? We are considered rogue now as well."

"But he handed a helpless woman over to an enemy."

Looking the other man in the eye, where he saw the depths of his shame and misery, Trent spoke coldly. "I'd say letting him live with that knowledge is the worst punishment he could suffer."

"Daily torture," Jaxon agreed quietly. "You know what's the most horrible part, though? She forgave me. Forgave me in that dirty fucking cell and then marked me as her mate. I deserved to die. Wanted to kill myself. And she told me it wasn't my fault and that she loved me." He ended on a broken whisper.

"So how did you and the girl escape? Because I am pretty sure I've seen that Bailey chick you're talking about back at the compound. Curly black hair, pregnant, hangs around with three big dudes."

Leaning forward, as if eager, Jaxon said, "So she didn't lose the baby? I wondered with everything that happened. Did she seem happy?"

"How the fuck would I know? I just said we saw her; didn't talk to her and learn her life fucking story."

"As long as she's safe," Jaxon muttered, easing back. "That's all that matters. I wasn't sure what happened after I jumped off the cliff. I didn't dare go back."

"Rewind there, buddy. What do you mean jumped off a cliff? Are you suicidal?" Trent wanted to stick his head in a cold bucket of water for clarity because the more he talked to this Jaxon guy, the more confused he got.

Jaxon laughed, a rusty sound with no mirth. "Nope, not suicidal, just determined to save the woman I love. Roderick, the vampire you don't want to believe in, had her prisoner. I fought his hold on my mind and did what I had to in order to save her. Bit him, which I don't recommend due to his foul taste, and when the fucker looked like he was going to get the upper hand again, I hugged him tight and threw us off a cliff."

"But you both survived?"

"Unfortunately. And I've been hunting the fucker ever since."

"Let's say for one second we believe this fellow's a vampire capable of controlling minds. Why the hell would you chase him knowing he can take over your will again?"

A vicious smile split the man's lips. "It seems the taste I got of his blood snapped his control, and he can't regain it. Although he's tried. Every time I get close, he tries to snare me—and fails. Even better, since that putrid taste, I always have a general feel for where he is. So, despite the fact he keeps moving, I keep following, taking shots at him when I get close enough, killing his minions when I come across them."

"And you thought we were his minions?"

"I'm not convinced you're not."

Trent leaned back on his heels, thoughtful. "Would his attempts at mind control feel something like a cold pressure on your head? Like something scrabbling to get in?"

Jaxon nodded. "Yes. There's pain, too. For those close enough, you can smell him, too."

"Like something dead and dark. I'm not saying I believe your story, but I did come across something like that. But he didn't take over my mind."

"He can't do it with the strong ones. And it could also be because I snuck up on him in this clearing and went for a headshot, but the fucker is fast. Before I could follow him, you came tearing through the woods with your buddies."

Marc frowned. "I thought I saw something whipping by, but it was so quick I thought I imagined it. But I'm wondering about something else you said. That whole minion thing. Are you implying he's got wolves working for him?"

"Not so much working as slaves to his will. Roderick can control weaker minds, take them over, and impose his will, although I'm sure some of them don't resist too hard. Evil is the easier path, and some I'm sure enjoy the blood and mayhem he asks them to cause."

"So my brother . . ." Trent closed his eyes and pinched the bridge of his nose. "My brother could be one of those minions then."

"I'd say that's likely."

Believing his brother might actually be a rogue meant Trent had to swallow the story about vampires and mind control. Yeah . . . He wasn't quite sure about that yet, no matter how much Jaxon seemed to believe and despite what he thought he'd felt. "Where are they holed up? I need to know."

"You want to confront Roderick and his wolves on their home turf?" Jaxon laughed. "I see I'm not the only one who doesn't care if he meets the reaper."

"If he's got my brother, I need to get him out."

"And there's a girl," Darren quietly added. "David took her with him when he disappeared into these woods. We don't know if she's still alive, but we should at least try and save her."

"Fuck, fuck, and fuck. Okay, listen here, I think I know the place they're hiding. I've been in these woods for about three days now, chasing down scent trails. There's only one area I haven't really explored, and that's up in the peaks. According to the ranger map I stole, there's an abandoned hunter's camp up there, about thirty or so miles from the closest starting point. By my research, it's got probably a half-dozen cabins, housing who knows how many wolves. Problem is getting up there without getting noticed is going to be a bitch. Not to mention, given the distance getting there and back before nightfall is going to be hard. I've been trying to draw the rogues out, wean his numbers so to speak, but Roderick's holding himself and his troops tight to the camp. Or was. I'm not sure what brought him out of hiding tonight."

Trent shifted. "Yeah, I think I have that answer. He was looking for fresh meat."

"You? Ha, like anyone would catch you off guard," Marc scoffed.

Trent looked at his toes, the sky, not willing to admit aloud his ignoble capture.

Darren punched him in the arm. "Holy fuck, someone did get the drop on him. How? Did they distract you with a hot chick?"

"Silver shot in the ass," he mumbled, "followed by a tranquilizer dart."

"Ouch, my man. Turn around and let us see." Marc laughed. "When I said we should get some scars, I was talking about manly ones, not new holes in your ass."

Trent shoved his friend. "Fuck off. This isn't funny. And that reminds me, there's a pair of hillbillies we need to catch because, if they're in cahoots with this Roderick prick, then they might have info."

Cracking his knuckles, Darren smiled. "Then let's go find ourselves some rednecks."

Without further ado, Darren and Marc shifted, one with a thick dark coat, the other, russet. They glanced at him as if asking, "What are you waiting for?"

Trent eyed the stranger and impulsively asked, "Are you coming with us?"

"After knowing I betrayed my pack and my mate, you would trust me to work with you?"

"I never said I trusted you, but we're both looking for the same target, so I'd be an idiot to not take all the help I can. Just so you know, though, fuck me over and I'll kill you myself."

"And just so you know," Jaxon said, a smile ghosting around his lips, "if you turn into an evil puppet wolf with red eyes, I'll keep your fur as a rug."

Their laughter rang through the woods. A dark mirth, but still, after a month of inaction, it felt good to be doing something, even if Trent planned to do it with a madman.

Chapter Three

Thea didn't know how long she'd existed in this prison. All she knew was Hell couldn't be any worse than this. She often lamented the stupid need for a chocolate bar that had driven her from the safety of her apartment to the corner store down the street. She played the what-if game in her head.

What if she'd eaten the crystalized ice cream in her freezer instead?

Or made some cookie dough?

Or gone to bed? Would she be living this nightmare if she'd just resisted the urge for chocolate? Would David still have snapped? And, if he hadn't, would she be living in her apartment with her possessed boyfriend, oblivious but safe?

Judging by the madman who held her captive—a psycho who controlled her former lover—nothing would have saved her. And she didn't doubt his mocking words when the creature with red eyes and the sharp teeth claimed no one would ever find her.

The shock of her capture, along with the discovery that monsters existed—vampires and werewolves and evil, oh my—should have made her lose the baby. Given her captivity and hopeless situation, she'd almost prayed for it.

But God didn't hear her. Instead, force-fed daily and exercised by wolves who nipped at her heels to keep her walking in circles around a dirt yard under a sky laden with stars, the baby grew, rounding out her stomach. She cupped her abdomen during the day, crying herself to sleep, praying for help. Locked in a moldy room with the windows boarded too tightly to let even a hint of light in, she despaired.

Who will find me? Does anybody care enough to even look? Thea hated these questions most of all because, with her parents dead and the rest of her family in Greece, strangers really, other than her landlord, who would give a damn?

The lonely answer hurt, and she suffered, even if no one physically harmed her. Lacking the power to do anything, she resorted to what she could. She tried to stop eating, the only method she could think of to escape. The vampire had her tied down, naked on a bed, thighs spread in offer. He brought in strangers, men whose eyes sparked with maliciousness or regarded her with blank apathy. Roderick gave her one warning. "Eat, or I'll let them fuck you." To emphasize his threat, he let their dirty, callused hands touch her. She begged for food in under a minute, the horror of his promise too much for her to bear.

"I thought you'd see things my way," he cackled. Roderick delighted in her captive state, detailing what he would do to her once he no longer needed her to bear the children who would form his army. He loved to show off his power and often marched in his minions, forcing them to do *his* will. He humiliated them then laughed as she cringed. Most didn't seem to care and eagerly obeyed his every decree. Weak cowards. Who cared if they clucked like a chicken or licked the floor for the vampire's entertainment?

The ones she hated seeing most were the ones who tried to fight *his* command.

"I've brought you a surprise, my breeding whore," Roderick said as his men dragged in a stranger. Tall and dark-haired, even with the bruises on his face, he appeared handsome—and defiant. "Meet Harrison. I'm about to teach him a new way of life. Kneel before your master, dog."

"Fuck you," said the oblivious newcomer. He even had the nerve to spit on Roderick, which had her silently cheering. Seconds later, he screamed on the floor as he tore at his own flesh, dragging his nails in sharp rivulets over his skin. Over and over, Roderick demanded the stranger kneel and accept his word as law. The man screamed instead. It seemed like an eternity, but was less than ten minutes, before Harrison, head hanging, blubbered, "I live to serve, master." So much for his pride.

Or how about Jeremy? He lasted longer than most. In other words, he defied Roderick for more than fifteen minutes.

"Crawl to me, dog. Lick my boots, and maybe I'll let you live."

"Bite me, you fucking undead freak."

A flick of the vampire's hands sent Jeremy to his knees screaming.

"Crawl and kiss the feet of the one who owns you," Roderick again commanded.

"Never! I won't be a slave." *Brave words that lasted about another hundred heartbeats while Roderick stared him down with his eerie red gaze. When Jeremy, wheezing and crying, finally slid across the floor and slobbered over Roderick's feet, the monster laughed. And laughed.*

The sound of his mirth often haunted her nightmares.

Those small spurts of bravery by newcomers pissed her off most of all because they gave her hope that someone could fight Roderick's control and rescue her. Kill the bastard who did this. It didn't happen. They all let her down, succumbing to the vampire's will. Cowards. Illogical and unfair of her, yet she couldn't help despising them for failing.

The one she abhorred most of all, though, the one she would never forgive, was David. *This is all his fault.*

As one of her captors, David often served her food, but no matter how she pled, he didn't respond in any way. There existed a blankness in his eyes, a jerkiness to his previously smooth movements. He was no longer the shy man she'd fallen in love with, but a shell, a shell possessed by *him*. Roderick. Vampire and monster. The one who loved to hear her beg and cry and scream.

The one who hurt her without laying a hand on her. The one who watched with an unholy hunger...

Despair became her only friend. Caught in a never-ending nightmare, she retreated into her mind, not speaking to anyone. Not reacting to Roderick's games. She just floated along, waiting for it to end, or so she thought until the well of resentment and frustration boiled over.

As part of his never-ending cruel joke, Roderick had David care for her. Actually, he was more like a robot who wore David's body and did his chores in absolute silence, neither happy nor sad. Not angry or confused. He did what he was ordered to. Until the day she snapped at him.

"How can you let him do this to me?" she screamed. "To our child?" She grabbed his hand and shoved it under her shirt, placing it against her rounded tummy. She barely felt the flutter of movement, but a shudder went through him.

For the first time since her capture, David looked her straight in the eye, his chiseled features and soft brown eyes still so handsome it seemed sacrilegious in this hellhole of a place. It seemed wrong that he remained attractive in the face of what he'd done. With his hand still on her stomach, his gaze turned so sad her lower lip trembled. This was the David she remembered. The one she'd fallen in love with a lifetime ago.

"Please, David. You need to get us out of

here."

Moisture pooled in his eyes. He licked his lips and spoke to her finally, only a handful of sentences, imbued with more meaning than anything she'd ever heard. "There is nothing to excuse what I did. I wish we'd never met, that I'd never hurt you. I wish I could have been stronger. If you ever escape, look for my brother, Trent. He'll give you anything you need. I am so sorry," he said in a voice that broke on the last word.

What was he sorry for? That he lacked the ability to save her? That he'd kidnapped her? Or that he was too scared to fix what he'd done wrong? "Don't be sorry. Help us, dammit. For the love of our unborn child, do something!"

"I can't." His cowardly reply didn't surprise her, but it still hurt.

"Can't or won't?"

"He'll hurt me if I try. I'm sorry, Thea. I never wanted this to happen. Please don't hate me."

Looking upon him, she noted the things she'd striven to ignore when they first met. While David appeared rugged on the outside, he wasn't the most assertive of men. It wasn't that he was a wimp. He could probably hold his own in a fight, but he complained a lot. Instead of making an effort to change the things that bugged him, like his job, he bitched and moaned. It was a trait Thea found most unattractive. *I like people who* know how to take responsibility for themselves. Who know how to stand up for what they believe in and fight for it. To be their own man or woman. David failed in all respects.

Once, she'd felt a spark for him. Love. But it wasn't enough for her to forgive him. His refusal to act and to do the right thing damned him. So, despite his plea that she not hate him—and his unspoken one asking for forgiveness—she remained silent, and his head drooped. Let him suffer; it couldn't come close to what she experienced.

Head bowed, feet shuffling, he moved away, but before he could exit the room, he halted. A cool breeze entered, its chill touch making her back away. She knew what it meant. Night had fallen, and Roderick watched.

Pivoting on one foot, David faced her, except David was no longer home. The puppet cocked its head, the red pinprick in his eyes still uncanny even after all this time. "Wasn't that touching? Or not. I can't say I blame you for not giving him forgiveness. Did he happen to mention that the only reason he ever went to meet you was so he could get you in bed? My doing, I admit. See, I learned something interesting with my other dormant experiments. It only works with a mated pair."

Her brow crinkled as the creature spoke to her. "What works?" she asked.

"In order for a dormant wolf to get pregnant

with a pup, she needs to have two things. The first you don't remember, but I assure you, you screamed deliciously. The second is she needs to be properly mated so that her wolf can stir. Simple really. But it has to be a true mating, not just any wolf bite will do. I actually threw a few of my flock your way, hoping for a match, but you ignored them all until pretty boy here."

"What are you talking about? I'm not a wolf like your other freaks."

"Such conviction, and yet so wrong. Look at the evidence. I'd say the results prove otherwise."

"What evidence?"

"The child you carry. One of the first to form my new army. I must say I am surprised you went for yellow-belly David over here. I expected you to hold out for one of my stronger subjects."

"So you planned this from the beginning?" she replied, bitter at the manipulation of her life.

"Planned, watched, and even participated. You didn't even notice the times I went along for a ride. You're a bit quiet for my taste, though."

Her stomach heaved at the knowledge. She clapped a hand to her mouth and shook her head, trying to deny it.

David's mouth tightened in displeasure, but it was Roderick who spoke, using his voice. "Bitch. If I weren't concerned about you losing the babe, I'd take you again, but this time I'd make you scream."

"Never."

The word didn't come from Thea, and her expression of surprise surely mirrored that on David's face. The red in his eyes was gone, and he trembled.

"David?"

"Thea. I—I—"

The monster himself came striding into the room, his displeasure not completely masked by his mocking smile. "Tsk. Tsk. You should know by now that I don't approve of my slaves revolting."

"Let us go," David demanded, his fierce tone at odds with his shivering frame.

"You can leave anytime. But she stays."

Confusion crossed David's face, but Thea whispered, "No," because she knew what Roderick meant.

The most horrifying part was David never even raised a hand to defend himself, but then again, how could he protect himself from . . . himself? He partially shifted into a beast that no longer made her scream. She'd seen them so often. Fingers tipped in claws, without a sound of protest or even an attempt to fight, David tore his own throat open. Blood gushed and spurted, torrents of it that sent her to her knees in numb disbelief.

I hated him . . . but I never wanted him to die.

Roderick held out his hand to capture the spray. He raised a bloody finger to his mouth and licked it. She gagged.

"Wasn't that fun?" he cackled.

Thea didn't answer, couldn't because, instead of cowering, fire burned inside her. David's death, while horrifying, didn't frighten her as intended. Instead it bolstered her resolve to escape. There was no one left to save her now but herself. She'd not even realized a part of her secretly hoped David would snap out of it and rescue her. Forget that. She could rely only on herself.

But I need to plan. There has to be a way to escape. A way back to the real world, freedom, and the cops. Actually, forget the men in blue. Someone needed to send her in the direction of a vampire hunter. Someone with a sharp stake and holy water to kill the monster that stole her life. *Someone strong enough to fight him and send him to hell, where he belongs.*

* * * *

It took them a day to actually track down the hillbillies. Their home-turf advantage aided them in hiding for longer than Jaxon's usual prey. Idiots with only half a brain between them, they should have left the woods entirely. Lycans with a purpose and a grudge made the worst enemies.

His new companion, Trent—so strange to hunt with others after all these months alone—found them and made them talk, after they'd finished screaming. But they didn't learn much other than a guy with freaky eyes had paid them to lure folks to their cabin. Once they had a victim, whom they were told to shoot with silver and tranquilize, they put up a flag on a tree and left. When they returned the next day, the body would be gone and a bottle of something alcoholic left behind.

Hoping to trap the hillbillies' patron, Darren ran the flag up the tree, and while they hid and waited, nothing came to take the bait. Or so Jaxon assumed. Not all of Roderick's minions acted liked red-eyed, rabid dogs. Jaxon himself acted normal for weeks before his ticking mental bomb exploded. It tempered his view toward the guys he'd befriended. *I hope I don't have to kill them.* But he would if he thought for a moment Roderick had his claws in them.

The hillbillies proved a dead end, and nothing came out to play, so they went back to the motel for a shower and to regroup.

"Dumb and dumber were useless," Marc quipped.

Trent paced. "We already guessed Roderick was paying them to lure victims for him, but even they weren't sure if he was holed up in that camp or not."

"So what's our next step?" Darren asked in his usual quiet tone.

Leaning back in a chair and trying to appear casual, Jaxon drawled, "Time to go meet the beast. Or his minions, at any rate."

"What happened to 'there's too many of them to fight'?"

"There is. Which is why I will act as a rabbit to draw them out while you three slip inside the camp, take care of the remaining rogues, and save the girl."

"You forgot to include rescue my brother."

Jaxon knew his gaze hardened. "I've already explained, if David's in that camp, then he's lost to you. Be prepared for that."

"You escaped."

"Did I?" Jaxon flashed a wan smile.

"I'll save him," Trent growled. "But as for your plan, what makes you think the rogues will give chase? Won't this Roderick have them on a tight leash?"

"His control is weaker during the day while he sleeps. Taunt the wolves enough, and some of them are guaranteed to come out and play. I just don't know how many. Are you prepared to kill if you need to?"

Trent shared a look with his friends then burst out laughing. "Buddy, we've never shied from violence, if that's what you're asking. We'll do what needs to be done."

"Then we go, first thing in the morning."

If they survived the night. Jaxon knew Roderick was aware of his presence. What surprised him was that the vampire hadn't come after him yet or sent his minions. What game did the monster play? Was he counting on Jaxon coming to him, knowing his need for vengeance?

I won't stop until he's dead. Until Bailey is safe. He wanted that more than anything. Hope for forgiveness didn't even enter the equation. How could he expect it when he would never forgive himself? But what he could give her and the pack he'd betrayed was a future free of Roderick. The right to live without fear.

This shining goal was the only thing that kept him going, from diving off a higher cliff in the hopes of never waking again.

Once the most carefree of wolves with a joke for everything, Jaxon had changed. Turned hard. Unrelenting.

He wondered if his old packmate Wyatt, who'd ever despaired of him taking anything seriously, would like the new him. Would he approve of the sober wolf Jaxon had become?

God, he missed his brothers, family by virtue of friendship and not blood. Wyatt, so cynical; Gavin, so strong and willing to do the right thing; and Parker, the gentle giant with the measured thoughts. He missed the camaraderie. The knowledge that he wasn't alone and someone had his back. Cast from the pack, Jaxon drifted alone.

In his adjoining room, he fell into a restless sleep, entering into his familiar nightmare, the horror of his actions overtaking him like it had every night since it happened.

Welcome to the origin of his shame. A dark cell in a hidden place. A room formed of cement blocks, mold, dust, and terror.

How did I get here? His thoughts were muddled. A shake of his head didn't clear the cobwebs, but he did become aware of a soft susurration that came not from the room but his head. He clutched his skull as the whisper turned into a blast of pain. Amidst the agonizing attack on his mind, he heard a chuckled, "Welcome, betrayer."

"No." He murmured the word. "No. No! NO!" The cry rose in intensity until he shouted it. *I am dreaming. I have to be.* Or he'd gone crazy. What else to explain the voice in his head?

A rustling of fabric froze his limbs. Still crouched, he pivoted, noting for the first time the pile in the dark corner. A focus of his senses and he could hear someone breathing. *I'm not alone.*

But who shared his prison? He inhaled deeply. Oh, no. The scent emanating from the limp form made his heart tighten. What had he done?

Images flashed in his mind as a floodgate hiding memories opened. He saw himself at the campsite so long ago with Bailey, the night she turned for the first time and attacked him. The night Roderick invaded his mind and made him his unknowing minion. Remembering made him pound the floor in frustration. How could he not have known the evil he harbored inside? Why couldn't he have fought harder?

Scrabbling on all floors, he hurried to Bailey's side. Kneeling by her, he held in a howl at the unavoidable evidence of his betrayal. "Bailey?" The uncertainty in his voice went well with his shame.

With a flutter of her lashes, she woke and stared at him. He flinched at the fury in her gaze.

"You!" She spat the word at him as she scrambled out of reach. "How could you do this?"

"Bailey—I—"

Engulfed in misery, he couldn't force any further words past his lips. Couldn't ask for forgiveness because he didn't deserve it. He'd hand delivered her to a monster. He deserved her hatred and anything else she chose to give him. Short of death, it wouldn't be enough.

"You betrayed your pack, Jaxon. Betrayed me," she cried, and he recoiled at each of her thrown accusations. Daggers straight to his heart.

She glared at him, expectant and deserving of an answer. "I didn't want to," he moaned, clutching at his hair and tugging it. "He got in my head. I had no choice. He controlled me. Oh, God, I wish Wyatt had killed me like he kept threatening. I should have died that night in the park."

"The night I attacked you?"

He nodded. A dormant Lycan raised in the human world, Bailey's wolf hadn't come out to play until she'd slept with her mate Gavin and the full moon forced her beast out. Mad with pain and terror, she'd attacked Jaxon. Not that he blamed her. The change wasn't an easy thing to handle and with her unexpected morph even worse. "Once Wyatt left to look for you, Roderick came out of the darkness. I tried to fight. I really did. But I was too weak, and he got into my head." He grimaced in remembered pain.

"Oh, Jaxon." Her tone softened. Sweet Bailey, how she deserved better than what he'd done.

"I didn't even remember until I woke up in this cell," he admitted with a mournful sigh. The monster had hidden his secret well. "I wondered why I kept dreaming of red eyes. I swear I didn't know what he'd done to me. As soon as you said you were pregnant, I wasn't me anymore. It was like I was a passenger while he drove. And he'd had me stash things, like drugs to knock you and the guards at the gate out." His shoulders shook as his head dropped to hide his tears of shame. "I wish I'd known. I would have killed myself before I hurt you or the pack," he whispered.

Sliding over to him, she put her arm around his shaking shoulders. "I know, Jaxon. He hurt me, too. And then made me forget."

"What does he want?"

She placed her free hand on her stomach. "He wants my child."

"But why?"

"Because he thinks my child is the key for him to build an army to destroy the packs."

"That makes no sense."

"I know, but don't forget, Roderick isn't all there."

"Tell me about it. I thought Wyatt was the coldest killer I know. This guy makes him look like a docile bunny rabbit."

"How long have we been here?"

"I don't know. At least a day. Maybe more. I remember driving for a long time before we got here." Long enough it would be hard to track them.

"Wherever we are, we need to get out."

Jaxon sprang up and went to the door, which of course didn't budge when he yanked on it. He pounded on it, frustrated and angry, the metallic echo dying slowly until silence reigned. *I need to get her out of here.*

"Save your strength," she cautioned. "We'll need to wait until he opens the door before we can make our move."

How optimistic of her. Resigned, Jaxon leaned against a cement wall and slid down. *I failed her.* Because of him, she'd endure torture, pain, and who knew what else at the hands of the vampire. He kept his gaze away from her. He didn't deserve to feast on her beauty. To bask in her regard. Why couldn't she have kept staring at him with hate? Why did she have to be so damned nice? He deserved to be whipped.

Beaten. Screamed at. Anything to punish him.

She ignored his body language, which screamed, "Stay away!" and sidled over until she sat beside him. He flinched when she laid her head on his shoulder. How could she stand to touch him after what he'd done?

"You know, I had your claiming all planned," she said softly.

"Y-you did?" His voice emerged hesitant. Once the guy with all the answers and jokes, he didn't know how to act. How to reply.

"Yup. I was going to bake a coconut cream pie."

"My favorite."

"I know. I figured you'd end up making some smart-ass remark, and I was going to throw my portion in your face."

A rusty chuckle made his frame shake. "What a waste of pie."

"Not really, because in my plan, you threw yours right back. And then"— she turned her head until she whispered against his ear —"I was going to lick it off you."

"You are a wicked girl, sweet cheeks," he said, turning until their lips hovered a hairsbreadth apart. He inhaled her scent, not understanding how she could still want to be close to him. How she could forgive him.

"I've been learning from the best," she said, letting herself lean in that last millimeter to touch his mouth. Their kiss was slow, sensual, and bittersweet. It brought tears to his eyes knowing that, despite what he'd done, she still cared for him. *I love you so much, Bailey.*

A part of him knew he should move away. He didn't deserve a reward, but she wouldn't let him go. She deepened the kiss as the thump of steps approached, and he couldn't find the willpower to push her away. Desperate for this last chance, he clung to her, and when she bit his lip, he wanted to shout because he knew she did it on purpose. She'd marked him. Despite everything, she wanted him as a mate. He managed to nip her back just inside the lip before the door burst open.

Blood hit his tongue. Opening his eyes wide, he stared into her equally alert gaze as the shockwave of their joining hit. It was done. He and Bailey were mated, no matter what happened next.

"Isn't this cozy?" a familiar, gravelly voice said with an evident sneer.

Bailey turned from Jaxon to face the monster. A need to protect suffused him. Jaxon pushed up off the floor and stood in front of her, every inch of him bristling with an instinct to keep her safe. "Let her go," he valiantly said.

A chuckle, which sent spidery tendrils to touch the edge of his mind, made him inwardly recoil, and Roderick's eyes glowed brighter. "Aren't you still just the comedian? Stand aside, boy. You've completed your task for the moment. I won't be needing you now until the bitch whelps. And wasn't that kind of you to bind her to you before I had a chance to order it?"

"What do you want with us?" Bailey demanded, standing to face their captor. God, how he loved her brave nature, even if she chose to exercise it at the most foolish of times.

"I want my own pack, of course. One not bound to me by force but because they're mine. Born and bred for one thing: to serve me."

"You're sick."

"I prefer to think of myself as a visionary. And you should thank me. As the mother of the future ranks, you get to live, along with the pup here who so kindly brought you. I'm sure he'll be more than happy to play stud."

"Never," Jaxon growled.

"Really?"

Roderick never moved, but Jaxon still dropped to his knees, screaming as he clutched his head. The pain... Hundreds of little nails getting driven into his skull.

"Stop it!" Bailey cried.

"Why? The sooner he learns my will is the only one he should own, the better." The agony increased, and Jaxon thought he would retch from it. How could anyone stand this level of pain?

An alarm sounded, startling them all. Roderick's face creased, and his eyes went blank.

Jaxon stopped screaming but still knelt on the floor, chest heaving, the lingering pain making it hard for him to focus. Sensing Roderick's inattention, Bailey grabbed at him and pulled. Jaxon stumbled to his feet, dizzy, his mind clouded. They didn't make it far. As she went to go around Roderick, the monster's hand shot out and grabbed her arm.

"Going somewhere?"

Bailey tugged but got nowhere. Still not quite recovered from the torture, Jaxon nevertheless lunged at Roderick. He never completed the move. With a scream of extreme agony, he clutched his head instead.

"Come, my pets, it's time to leave. It would seem my son and his ragtag rabble of dogs have stumbled upon us."

As Roderick dragged Bailey, Jaxon's mate and one true love, down a corridor lit by bulbs dangling from strings, Jaxon howled for her. *Stumbled to keep up, arms stretched to stop her, to save her...*

Jaxon lunged up from the mattress, reaching for Bailey. And grasped only thin air. The ache in his heart matched his tears. Once he would have laughed at a man who cried, but now, now he just wished he could find a way to stop the hurt.

Kill Roderick. It's the only solution. Kill the one who took away his life and his love. *Maybe if I kill enough, the pain will finally go away.*

Chapter Four

Hugging her superbly large stomach, Bailey waddled to the front porch her mates had built her and surveyed them as they worked on their newest present to her—a gazebo. She still hadn't quite figured out what one did with the octagonal structure, but she didn't tell them that, not when they seemed so darned determined to give her one. Boredom plus power tools made for some interesting projects, she'd discovered.

Next on their agenda, they'd informed her, was a play structure for the baby. Never mind the child wouldn't be big enough to play on it for at least a year or more. Apparently their child would need one. And the list went on.

Truly, though, she couldn't complain. How many women had three men determined to make her life as wonderful as possible? Sometimes she couldn't believe her luck, but as her new best friend, Dana, had said, "Three is so much better than one. Especially all at once."

But in her mind, four was the magic number.

Absently, she ran her tongue over the inside of her bottom lip, the small, ridged scar from the bite Jaxon had given her—their mating exchange—tingled again. *Where are you, my missing mate?* She'd told her guys about binding with

Jaxon in the cell. They'd accepted it and then never spoken of it again. Betrayal wasn't something they would forgive. However, she found it harder than them to forget the man with the beautiful smile and dancing green eyes. She relived over and over his death, his final words. She dreamed of him sometimes, calling to her, his spirit so broken and despairing. She woke from those dreams shivering, allowing whichever man she slept with to comfort her.

What she didn't tell her men was her belief that Jaxon lived—along with Roderick. Truthfully, she was pretty sure they already suspected given the fact they never let her out of sight and the way the security for the compound had never abated, even after that final battle.

A part of her knew with a certainty that bore no foundation except her gut that one day Roderick, that evil creature, would return. But next time, she'd be prepared for him. She went everywhere with a sharpened stake and vial of holy water. And she wasn't alone.

The pack would eventually have their revenge.

But what about Jaxon? What would happen to her fourth mate when the monster was defeated? He'd betrayed the pack by handing her over to the vampire. Anger at him would have been the logical choice. Her mates certainly had no problem hating him. She didn't find her own emotions that eager to join the "Hate Jaxon

Club." Instead, she missed him and his easy smiles. Hated knowing that even if Roderick were killed, Jaxon wouldn't be accepted back into the pack. Lycans weren't the most forgiving bunch. If Jaxon did survive and they eventually put the horror behind them and vanquished the monster, how could she get them to take her fourth mate back?

Gavin, Wyatt, and Parker loved her, and, oh, how she loved them, too. When it came to her safety, though, they were absolutely psycho, especially with the baby getting so big in her belly, the flutters of its kick felt when they placed their palms on her taut skin.

Even if the pack forgave Jaxon, her mates never would. They would never trust him—a dilemma she worried about, even though she didn't yet have proof her fourth mate lived. *I know in my heart he does, though. And he's fighting, fighting for a way to remove the danger to me. To redeem himself in my eyes. I just wish I could tell him that he doesn't have to. I love him no matter what happened in the past.*

She just hoped she got a chance to tell him.

* * * *

With Jaxon's caution about Roderick and his mental powers ringing in his ears, crazy as it sounded—*like I'm going to believe in a mind-controlling vampire-Lycan*—Trent waited by the edge of the woods with his friends. The stink of wolves who'd foregone bathing and something acrid, a stench borderline putrid and yet somehow familiar, burned his nose and made his beast fidget in his mind. But he couldn't shift, not yet. He'd need hands to open the doors. However, just in case, he was ready to go furry, stripped naked with his clothes tucked up a tree. Someone with a video camera would have a blast if they saw him tiptoeing through the underbrush, his man parts swinging free. Lycans, though, would think nothing of it because nudity was a regular part of life. After all, the budget for new clothes only went so far.

So, naked as the day of his birth, he waited for the signal. Darren and Marc also waited in their own spots, silent and covered in a hunter's perfume—a.k.a. fucking animal piss, which made his eyes burn—to mask their scent. For a wolf, hiding seemed almost shameful. Trent preferred bold actions and straight-up confrontations. Looking his target in the eye then ripping out their throat. Of course, in the past, most of his victims were dumb animals, but still, even when he'd joined those rogue hunts and helped take down Lycans, babbling freaks who practically foamed at the mouth, he'd preferred the straight-up kill, the kind where he could look his target in the eye to the option of taking them out from afar via sniper.

Lycans fought and killed by the claw. Except

for Jaxon, who'd tucked his gun, loaded with silver bullets, into his pants with a taunted, "In the war of numbers, I prefer to even the odds."

Trent still had a hard time believing everything Jaxon claimed. A vampire controlling wolves. A bunch of crazy rogues all working together. It didn't seem likely. But the closer they got to the abandoned hunting camp—a grueling eight-hour trek uphill that involved them wading in water to muddle their route, constantly spraying themselves to avoid detection, killing two sentries they found wandering—the more he couldn't deny the number of scent trails. A dozen, eighteen, more than twenty. *Shiiiiit. That is a lot of fucking carnivores in one place.*

Maybe Jaxon's plan to draw them off and kill a few with his shiny gun wasn't so preposterous, if he managed to get them to come out and play.

As he waited, Trent listened for the promised distraction. He almost smiled when he heard it.

"Hey, you mangy, fucking furballs. I hear Roderick's been looking for me," Jaxon shouted brazenly as he strutted up to the edge of the camp. "Here I am. Now, who's still got enough balls to try and catch me? Hell, to make it sporting, I'll even stay in my human shape."

At first there was no answer, although Trent caught a flicker of movement at one of the intact windows.

"Meow. Meow. Here, pussy-pussies. Are you all too busy chasing your tails?" Jaxon made more cat noises. Still nothing. What would he try next?

Oh, he didn't! He did! Trent held in a chuckle as Jaxon whipped his dick out and pissed on the ground, whistling merrily as he let his spray dance in the dirt, probably spelling his name. And that finally made the rogues snap. If there was one thing they couldn't stand, it was another marking their territory.

A snarl sounded, followed by several more of varying pitch. With a taunting laugh and a jiggle before he stuffed his dick away, Jaxon ran into the woods, a stream of wolves, eleven by Trent's count, slavering and snapping after him.

I hope he knows what he's doing. A sharp crack and a yelp later, he shook his head as the crazy wolf with a death wish gave them the diversion they needed to sneak in.

Trent swung out of the tree, landed on sure feet, and ran at the biggest cabin. In the center of camp and ringed by the other smaller huts, it seemed the logical choice to start with. He didn't make it far before furry bodies flew out of abruptly opened doors and smashed windows.

The fight was on.

Shifting into his wolf, glad he'd stripped beforehand—because a wolf wearing tighty whities just didn't inspire the right level of fear—he dove into the madness with ferocious glee. A month's worth of frustration boiled over as he bit and clawed at the bodies pummeling him. See a neck? Bite down hard. Feel movement? Duck. Catch one trying to tuck tail and run? Pounce and take him down.

In the heat of battle, his blood coursing through his frame, he caught only glimpses of the chaos around him. What he saw assured him that his two friends had joined the fray to tear and maim anything that thought to attack.

It was with a sense of relief that Trent noticed none of the wolves who'd first chased Jaxon or the ones currently trying to rip his throat out were his brother. What he would have done if his little bro attacked remained a mystery. But he did know what he planned to next. Find him.

Don't worry, David, big brother is here, and I'm going to save you and the girl before I kick your ass for scaring the shit out of me.

* * * *

A shouting voice woke her, and Thea lay in bed wondering if she'd imagined it. In the daytime, things tended toward the quiet and she used that time to sleep, not always an easy feat with the sunshine they denied her heating the cabin and rendering her room, with its boarded-up window, stifling. She rolled over on the mattress, ignoring its poking springs and brown stains, and closed her eyes.

Doors slammed in the hall, accompanied by excited snarls. Hmmm, sounded like something had provoked the freaks keeping her captive. Maybe a giant bunny hopped into the camp. Or someone had come back with dog treats from the store.

She tuned out the cacophony and shifted yet again, looking for a nonexistent, comfy spot. So long as they didn't bother her, she really didn't give a damn. Thea didn't stir even when she heard the commotion arrive right outside her door. Why bother? Energized by David's death, she'd looked for a way out. Fought to no avail. All it gained her was Roderick's sick attention— and that wasn't something to aspire to. It was easier to give up again. With David dead and the madman in charge, forget any rays of sunshine. She'd inhabited this hellhole long enough for the cops to find her, if they'd even bothered to look. As for escape, even if they accidentally left the door unlocked, her hard, rounded belly couldn't exactly handle the hard run that she'd need to escape wolves.

Now there was a shocker right up there with the vampire. Who would have thought the legends of people turning into slavering beasts was true? She certainly hadn't, but she changed her mind quickly the first time one of the rancid-smelling bastards shed his clothes and turned furry. The howl wasn't the eeriest part nor the stomach churning she endured as she watched limbs reshape themselves and fur sprout. No, the worst thing was the eyes and seeing the intelligence, that oh-so-human awareness, mixed with madness, watching her. Tracking her every movement. *It's just not right.*

Then again, knowing werewolves existed, along with bloodsucking undead freaks, paled in comparison to another discovery. According to the vampire, she was a monster, too, a decree she refused to believe. Roderick was a liar who loved to say things, shocking things, to watch the reaction of his victims, soaking in their terror and misery. So his announcement, she'd one day turn furry on the full moon? No way was she swallowing that one. *I'd know if I wasn't human, wouldn't I?* Of course she would. But she couldn't help thinking of David. David was a werewolf, so what did that make her baby?

The door flung open and hit the wall with a crash, derailing her thoughts. Startled at the intrusion, she could help but swivel and she saw a man in the door. And what a man. Naked, he had a tanned and smooth body, and he rippled with muscles as he stalked into the room. It was enough to make her breath catch however, good-looking or not, his state of undress could mean only one thing: he was a wolf.

She backed away from him, huddled into the corner, and tucked her knees up, protecting her belly. The startling blue gaze, one she'd not met before, took her in, his eyes scanning her frame. She couldn't miss how his already half-erect cock twitched, and she flinched. Had the vampire lost the leash on his dogs? Was this stranger here to rape her? Kill her? A whimper escaped her as she wrapped her arms tighter around herself, a protective measure that would do nothing if he decided to attack.

"Thea?" His knowledge of her name did nothing to abate her fear. He reached out a hand, a big one with long, callused fingers, and if she could have merged with the wall, she would have.

"Go away," she whispered, caving to fear. "Please. Don't hurt me."

His dark brows drew together, but before he could reply, he whirled to meet an attacking furry body. The mottled wolf snarled and snapped at the stranger. They grappled, their struggle taking them out of the room to ricochet in the hall.

What the hell was going on? Why were they fighting each other? Were they allies or enemies? He knew her name. Could he have come to rescue her?

Unlikely given he was a wolf, too. It seemed more likely he'd gotten caught trying to play with the vampire's prisoner and now paid the price.

Forget the handsome man with the startling blue eyes, though. The door! He'd left it wide open. A trick? Or a mistake?

On bare feet, she crept to it, flinching at every crash and snarl, expecting at any moment for someone to come hurtling through that door and yank her precious hope of escape away. She made it to the doorjamb and froze. She peered around the edge and noted the empty hall. The sound of fighting echoed still, but it appeared to have moved elsewhere.

One step. Two. By the third she was walking quickly, unsure of where to go where they wouldn't recapture her, but she was determined to try. An exit. She needed an exit. Or a big window. Anything to get her outside.

A naked man, a different one, sporting short red strands, freckles, and slabs of muscles blocked the end of the corridor. Friend or foe? She didn't wait to find out. She darted into an open doorway and quickly slammed the door shut. But would the flimsy portal suffice? She slid a dresser with peeling paint across it and panted from the exertion as she looked around.

No other doors graced the room, but she spotted an unboarded window. A yank on the sash accomplished nothing. Time and humidity had warped the frame. The doorknob behind her jiggled, and she heard voices murmuring.

I need to get out. How the outdoors would prove any better, she refused to think on. One step at a time. First, get out of the room. Then . . . she'd wing it.

There wasn't much in the room to use as a weapon, but an old chair provided just the right momentum to smash through the dirty glass. *Oh, crap, that was noisy.* And if the silence on the other side of the door was an indication, it didn't go unnoticed. She ignored the few remaining shards as she scrambled out the window, hissing as one pointed piece sliced across the side of her thigh and left a lengthy gash. Ignoring the welling blood, she hopped to the pine needle–laden ground. Not stopping to get her bearings or look around, instead she quickly walked, her bare feet protesting the rough ground, her heart hammering in her chest.

I'm outside. Unbelievable. She'd made it that far. It seemed like a miracle. The edge of the woods beckoned, but she halted as a silver-coated wolf with red eyes stepped into her path.

It stalked her, its lip peeled back in a snarl as it trod toward her on big, hairy paws. She retreated, flicking a glance to the side, only to see another furry beast with an equally violent expression. The other side proved open, and despite knowing she couldn't outrun the fleeter creatures, she tried. She hugged her belly as she jogged, her captivity and lack of firm muscle tone before the kidnapping working against her. The wolves gave chase, snarling and growling. To her credit, she said not a word, more because she couldn't, each indrawn breath a sharp, wheezing pain.

A yelp sounded behind her, and she couldn't prevent herself from craning to look. A third wolf with dark fur had arrived, and he battled the two chasing her. God, the savagery of it. She didn't ogle the violence long because she smacked into something hard and bounced back. Hands reached out to grab her arms, steadying her as she turned back to see who'd caught her and ended her short-lived escape.

The face she saw hit her like a punch to the gut. Golden-haired, his lip bloody, and familiar brown eyes alight with ferocity, he stood there, and she sucked in a breath. It couldn't be.

"David?" Her soft query didn't go unheard.

"No. I'm his brother, Trent. I'm here to save you. Both you and David. Do you know where he is?"

His brother? She stared closer. The resemblance she'd initially espied resided on the surface only, she realized. Although Trent and David shared the same thick blond hair and brown eyes, even the same general face structure, everything about this man was bigger, harder, from his expression to his body. In other words, he looked like a meaner version of David, which wasn't reassuring. She cringed from him and held out her hands in a plea.

"Please don't hurt me."

His brows shot up, and his expression turned grimmer. "I wasn't intending to. Just what happened here?"

Happened? What hadn't? A hysterical bubble of laughter threatened to burst free, and she bit the inside of her cheek to halt it. He held out a hand and beckoned. She stood frozen instead. Naked like the other men she'd encountered, he was a wolf, too, or so she could only assume—*just like his brother.* The knowledge didn't reassure.

Impatience darkened his eyes. "Come on, we need to go! I doubt the diversion is going to last long, and I don't have the numbers to hold them off if they come back."

Escape? With him? She peered back at the battling wolves, now down to two, with the scruffy one who'd initially confronted her lying prone on the ground.

"Don't worry about Darren. He'll keep that rogue off our back."

"You're here to save me?" She couldn't help the incredulity in her tone.

He nodded and again held out his hand.

Because she doubted she'd get a better offer, and despite his overwhelming presence, she inched toward him, ready to flee at the slightest hint of madness in his face—or red in his eyes, the precursor for the evil to come.

The shock when he clasped her hand traveled up her arm and made her eyes widen. She'd felt a smaller version of it with David. How odd his brother caused the same reaction. He didn't say if he felt it, too, just tightened his fingers around hers and tugged her after him.

"We have to hurry. Tell me where they're keeping David. We need to grab him and get out of her."

She blurted out the truth. "He's dead."

The body tugging hers stumbled before he

caught himself. He wheeled around. "He's what? How? Are you sure?"

"I had a front-row seat. The monster made him kill himself in front of me."

There was no mistaking the shocked daze in his eyes. "David would never commit suicide."

"David would have done anything to escape *its* control." Yes, she sounded bitter. It was hard to respect a man who would rather kill himself than fight to live and save his child. She didn't care how fucking strong the creature called Roderick was. It still seemed cowardly to her.

The brief glimpse of grief in Trent's eyes disappeared, replaced by a hard glint. "You will tell me the whole story, but first let's get out of here. Follow me."

Did she have a choice?

At the sound of howling, a chorus of it echoing from the woods, he darted into a cabin, the front door hanging off its hinges. He led her through the trashed living room into a filthy kitchen, the cupboards wide open, those with doors at any rate, the sink full of dishes swarming with a haze of flies. The bright sunlight streaming through the windows made her blink as it decided to burst out from behind the clouds. Trent didn't give her time to adjust or think, yanking her after him across the torn linoleum floor and out an already open door. They hit the porch, never slowing, and he emitted a piercing whistle.

Who did he signal? She didn't have time to wonder as a pair of wolves came loping around the corner. She shrieked and pulled back against the hand anchoring her. He didn't let go, nor did he slow down, heading straight to the hairy pair and talking to them.

"David's dead, but I found the girl. We need to get out of here."

An ululation rose from her left where a thick line of trees marched off into the distance, a symphony of howls that started with one and ended in a chorus.

Trent, who kept his hand glued to hers, lifted his head and sniffed the air.

"They're coming back. Fuck. Thea, right?" he asked, pinning her in place with his gaze.

She nodded.

"We're going to have to run, okay? As fast as you can."

"I take it that's not more of your friends coming?"

"Not exactly. More like nasty wolves with sharp teeth. Probably the same ones that have been keeping you captive. And I doubt they're going to be happy we've shown up and stolen you."

Good enough. At least he didn't try to sugarcoat it. "What about them?" she asked, inclining her head to his furry buddies.

"The least of your worries. Trust me. You need to come with me if you want to live."

With freedom a sudden possibility and with a chance to save her unborn child, Thea ran like the wind, or her version at any rate. Unfortunately, it wasn't fast enough.

Chapter Five

Trotting on four feet behind Trent and the female they'd saved, Darren tried to process everything that had happened in the last few minutes. And he didn't mean the battle.

When he'd kicked open the door to the only barred room he'd found in the large cabin, he'd not expected the kick to the gut when he saw the small brunette peering fearfully at him. She had reason. Enclosed in a dark room with only a bed to sit on, a bed with currently unused restraints hanging at the four corners. A wild rage imbued him, a rage that grew as he noted her fear. Then he got a whiff of her, and even unbathed and frightened, her underlying scent, the odor that marked every person like a fingerprint, hit him, and his eyes widened further in surprise. His wolf roused enough to growl, *Mine*.

Unfucking believable. He'd found his mate.

Darren wanted to gather her in his arms, reassure her that she was safe. Instead, he'd gotten attacked by yet another fucking rogue. The place virtually crawled with them, but lucky for his crew, the attacking rogues, crazed and slavering creatures, were made clumsy by their madness and had been thus fairly easy to dispatch. They did, however, have numbers on their side. Did they ever, which meant he needed to quickly take care of his current attacker before reinforcements arrived. But he didn't want to frighten Thea further with the bloody violence required to put the snapping rogue down. Despite what his wolf wanted—*protect the female!*—he led his attackers away.

When he returned, no worse for wear, he found the room empty and his mate gone. Following her scent led him to a closed door, where Marc stood, looking puzzled.

"She ran away from me." He sounded incredulous. "I thought when you rescued a damsel they were supposed to throw themselves at the man and thank them for being their hero? A nice thank-you kiss? Or a promise of a bj for later?"

Darren resisted an urge to punch his friend, especially for doing what came naturally. Since their teens, they'd quite enjoyed ribald jests and comments aimed at the fairer sex. But with it now aimed at Thea, Darren no longer saw the humor. Not one bit. "You're an idiot. The girl is terrified, and here we are, naked as the fucking day we were born, wolves all over the place, covered partially in blood. I'd be freaking, too."

"That's because, somewhere down the line, one of your ancestors fucked a pussy."

Darren ignored his friend to grab the doorknob and turn.

"Don't bother. She slid something across it."

"We breaking it down?"

"We could, or we could come into the room from outside, where she's not expecting us."

The tinkling sound of glass breaking spurred them into action. They ran back to the kitchen area and dove out the back door—or at least Darren did. Marc got halted by another rabid wolf coming out of nowhere.

Help his friend or go after the girl? Darren kept going. She needed him more than Marc did. It took him just a second to spot Thea running, not very quickly, while a pair of rogues chased her. *Fuck!* Still recovering from his last shift not even five minutes ago, he nevertheless morphed into his other shape and took off after the enemy, his long legs eating up the ground. With a soaring leap, he tackled the lead one. Lucky for her, the other one stopped to help his buddy. Two against one?

Easy odds. His wolf practically slobbered in glee with the blood and action it got to enjoy. But he didn't have time to play with his prey. Kill them quickly, grab the girl, and get out of there before the rest came back.

A crunch of bone, a yelp of pain, and a few shakes of his head; he took care of the rogues, one dead weight on the ground, the other wheezing as its life force seeped from a neck wound. Lifting his muzzle, he scanned the area, only to find her gone. As he loped in the direction in which he'd last seen her scurrying, he caught the scent of bear piss, Trent's perfume for this invasion. Relieved she didn't flee alone, he tracked the smell, his short yip answered by Marc.

Darren caught up to them as they fled the camp, minus David, but plus one female. As he took on the role of rear guard, his mind mulled over the rapidly unfolding events. With his wolf currently driving, he couldn't ignore the possessive urge coursing through him as he watched Thea's ass wiggle under the thigh-high shapeless gown she wore. Rounded calves; full bottom; short, not even chin-high, he bet she cleaned up nicely. *But she's not a wolf.* Or so his nose claimed. Yet despite her human status, she drew him. Called to his beast. *I've found my mate.* What else could explain the instant connection he felt for her?

The idea didn't scare him. He'd waited almost twenty-seven years to encounter a woman who made his wolf howl. Who made him want to put downs roots and start a family. But he needed to slow down. They were strangers. All he knew currently was her name—and the fact that she possessed a wicked wiggle—but their stranger status didn't bother him. Part of the excitement involved getting to know her and finding out what fate had in store. First, though, he'd have to aid her in getting over her abduction and abuse. That terrified look she sported when he first saw her flashed to mind. *I'll have to take it real slow and careful.*

Speaking of slow. Watching her move, a slow, stumbling trot, as she tried to keep up with Trent, who yanked her along, he was the first to notice how she panted heavily. Something seemed amiss. He loped up to place himself alongside her and noted how she clutched her middle with her free hand, a tummy more rounded than expected, given the size of her legs and arms. However, it was the scent of her blood and the view of it running down her one leg, and more of it coating her soles that had him shifting despite his fatigue.

With quick strides, he came up alongside her, and swung her into his arms—where she belonged. *Fuck*, the tingling awareness that shot through him almost had him stumbling in shock. If he'd harbored any doubt, it disappeared. *No two ways about it, she's mine.*

"What the fuck are you doing?" Trent asked, still holding her hand.

"She's injured and can't keep up."

"So you're going to carry her the whole way down the mountain?" Trent snarled, seeming displeased for some reason. Actually, a good reason seeing as how they'd come away without their main purpose: David. Or was there more at play here, given he seemed reluctant to release his grip?

"I'll carry her to the motel if I have to," Darren replied, tightening his grip. "She's not like us."

"No shit, Sherlock. But we've got about thirty miles to cover. You aren't going to be able to carry her the entire way while outrunning the rogues."

"Watch me! Besides, it's mostly downhill from here."

"Please don't fight. I'll walk," she interjected.

"We need to run!" Trent snapped.

Darren's jaw tightened at the fear in her tone. "Stop scaring her, Trent. I understand your brother's gone and you're upset, but don't punish her for it."

"I wasn't." Trent grimaced as he released her hand. "Fine. You want to carry her then be my fucking guest. But we need to hurry. It looks like Jaxon's ruse failed, or he's dead. The other wolves are coming back." As if to reinforce Trent's claim, howls echoed behind them. Darren increased his pace to a steady jog, finding a reserve of strength inside that stemmed from a need to protect his precious burden.

Thea bounced in his arms, and she clung to him as he jogged. *As if I'd let her fall.* Not while he still breathed.

Foliage crackled around them as they chose speed over stealth. Despite his added burden, Darren kept his gait steady for the first mile, even if the urge to sprint kept nudging him every time he heard a howl. A flat-out run this far from the truck would just wind him and sap his energy.

"Why are you doing this?" she asked, her voice low so as to not carry.

"Doing what?" he asked, keeping his answer short so as to not waste breath.

"Carrying me? Risking your life?"

Was it too soon to say because he intended to claim her as his forever? Probably. "You're not that heavy. And I've always wanted to be a hero."

"Heroes save princesses. I'm not that special."

"I beg to differ. My name, by the way, is Darren."

"Can you save the chitchat for later, when we're not in mortal danger?" Trent barked.

"He's right. We're in terrible danger. We need to be far away from here before sundown," she whispered, the haunted look in her eyes returning. "Put me down. You'll just slow yourself down by carrying me."

"And what of the baby you carry?" Darren asked, suddenly sure of his suspicion, as she cradled her rounded belly still and had since he'd scooped her up.

"How did you know?" Brown eyes framed in dark lashes peered up at him. He couldn't wait until he could make their expression a happier one.

"What baby?" Trent asked. He stopped dead. "Whose baby?"

Thea's eyes closed, and Darren, closest to her, almost didn't hear her answer. "David's."

Fuck.

Baby or not, the view of his wolf didn't change. *Mine. Ours. Protect the pup.* Since that coincided with his own feelings on the matter, he ignored Trent's dazed look and forged ahead. Moments later, Trent took point, back in his wolf shape, his enhanced senses leading the way to the creek, their stash of supplies, and, if lucky, safety.

Behind him, he could sense Marc guarding the rear. Flanked by his two best friends, Darren ran, ignoring the sharp stones that bit into his feet. Forget heading back to the cache where he'd left his stuff a mile outside of the camp. They needed out of here as fast as possible. He just hoped they didn't run into any humans or park rangers. A naked man carrying a bleeding, missing woman accompanied by wolves might be a touch hard to explain. Add in a semi-hard cock that refused to pay attention to the dire situation because her scent enveloped him, and, well, he'd probably go straight to jail—*no passing go, no collecting nothing.*

And that wouldn't work for him, not with his future resting in his arms. Protecting Thea from everything, even well-meaning humans, now took precedence over everything else. The mating fever had him in its grasp, and Darren didn't intend to fight it.

A warning yip from up ahead preceded a black wolf swerving in from the side. It took only a moment for Darren to realize Jaxon had joined them. It changed nothing. He kept pumping his legs, watching for obstacles and leaping over them. The body in his arms jostled, but to her credit, Thea didn't complain, although she did hold on for dear life. *Now if only we were naked, with a bed and a little privacy. I'd give her a different reason to hold on tight.* Such an inappropriate thought for the current situation, but as a goal, it kept him moving even when fatigue threatened to slow him down.

The first attacking wave consisted of only a pair. While his pack brothers took care of them, Darren kept going and Jaxon dropped back to cover his rear. It bothered him to run from a fight. However, this was one of those times where the safety of an innocent—*my mate*—mattered more than his bloodlust.

A shape came leaping from the side, the sound of their own flight having masked its approach. He spun, and the fur of the attacking wolf brushed his side. With a snarl, Jaxon engaged the beast, and Darren managed about thirty more paces before a sixth sense had him dumping Thea on the ground and whirling to meet an opponent. The creature shifted as it came, a scream of pain and rage echoing through the woods.

"Fucking bastards. Give her back!" the sandy-haired man in his late thirties or forties screamed at him with wild eyes.

"You want her, come and get her," he

taunted with crooked fingers.

"You don't know what you've done. He'll kill you for this if you're lucky. Make you one of us if you're not."

"I'm not scared of some undead creature. If he even exists. Maybe you and your buddies are just fucked in the head. Sick with rabies or some other Lycan disease."

An almost-sad smile crossed the unshaven man's face. "I wish. Because then I would have hope. You should have walked away." He spoke his quiet warning and the male's eyes changed, with the lucid light being overtaken by a red hue. His lips opened wide in a feral smile, and he charged.

Darren met him, punch for punch. The other man moved fast, but Darren didn't play nicely. When he saw his chance, his foot came up and nailed the guy in the sac. As the other man recoiled, Darren reached and grabbed his head before dropping to the ground in his favorite modified wrestling move. The snap let him know the fight was done.

After he let go of the limp body, he stood and looked around. Thea hadn't remained where he'd dropped her, but he quickly found her, her blood and scent trail too easy to follow. He heard her breathing from behind a large tree and said, "It's me. Don't be frightened. He's gone."

"You—you killed him?"

The truth seemed best. "Yes. Does it frighten

you?"

"No. He wasn't a nice man."

"Then I'm glad he's dead. Anyone else you'd like me to take care of?"

She peered around the trunk, her brown eyes curious. "Why would you do that for me? You heard him. Roderick's going to come for you. All of you. He's not going to let me go."

"Then he'll have to go through me because I'm not giving you back. I will protect you, Thea."

"No one can protect me from him."

"We'll find a way. Will you let me try?"

He held out his hand. Logic and his wolf howled that he needed to grab her and continue to run. But the man—whose heart stopped as he waited for her answer—wanted to earn this first step in her trust. To his relief, she emerged from behind the tree and clasped his hand.

Despite her being dirty, bedraggled, her hair standing on end, her eyes wide and still frightened, he'd still never seen a more beautiful sight. *Ours.*

* * * *

As she was clasped in the man's arms and held on to his neck as he ran once again, Thea wondered if she'd gone mad. When he'd said, "I will protect you, Thea," a part of her actually believed him. Trusted him when he said he'd find a way. Did it have to do with the spark she felt when he first touched her, a spark she'd felt to a smaller extent with David then, more shockingly, his brother, Trent. Did she want to believe because he spoke with such conviction and honesty in his eyes? Or was it the odd voice in her head, a voice she'd heard only recently that said he would protect them. That he belonged to them. *He is ours*, the voice whispered. *Trust him and the light-furred one. They are . . .* Thea didn't understand the next word because it was more of an image, a group of wolves, really, running, together like a big, furry family.

Madness. Her captivity and pregnancy hormones had obviously overtaken common sense. One, normal people didn't hear voices. And two, she didn't know these guys. Although they seemed hell-bent on helping her escape, that didn't mean she could automatically trust them no matter what the little voice in her head said. Who was to say they didn't want her for nefarious reasons?

Somehow I think their intentions are honorable. Her gut just knew from the way they seemed determined to protect her against horrible odds to the way the one named Darren carried her so gently. Only time would truly tell.

She didn't know how long they ran, but she could certainly admire his stamina, as his pace never let up, despite the way his heart pounded in his chest. From time to time, his wolf friends would join them, only to veer off when the approaching sound of snarls and crackling bushes alerted them to an imminent attack.

It seemed as if they would run forever, chased and fighting. But suddenly they spilled onto a riverbank or creek—she wasn't sure, given it wasn't superbly wide, maybe twenty, thirty feet, but flowed rapidly over rocks downhill.

The russet wolf joined them and shifted. She averted her eyes from his nudity, but still got a glimpse of pale skin covered in freckles.

"Hand her over," said the stranger who'd shadowed their mad flight.

Panicked, she clung to Darren.

"I've got her," Darren replied as he gave her a reassuring squeeze.

"You're slowing down. Give yourself a break and let me carry her for a bit. We can switch back again when we reach the cache at the forked tree."

She could feel the reluctance in Darren's body. He didn't want to let her go, and she didn't want to leave the haven of his arms. But she also knew how tired he had to be after their flight.

"I'll walk," she announced. As if to mock her, a howl rose from behind them from the shadowy copse of trees.

"Be careful with her, Marc," Darren said gruffly. "She's pregnant."

The redhead rolled his eyes. "I won't let her bun in the oven come to any harm. Now hand her over so we can get going again. The water will only stall them for so long. I can't believe we haven't lost them yet considering the eau de pee-pee we're wearing."

"They're following her scent. Or were. I think the blood she was dripping has stopped now that her wound's clotted."

"I hope so because there's still way too many of them." Marc held out his arms and waited.

Darren sighed. "I'm sorry, honey, but Marc's right. I need to recuperate a little. Don't be scared. I know he's not as good-looking as me, and smells like a pregnant doe right now, but he's harmless. And I'll be right beside you."

"Next time I get to wear the raccoon piss while you wear the aroma of pregnant prey."

"He who sprays gets first choice," Darren taunted. To her surprise, he pressed a chaste kiss on her forehead before he handed her over.

"See you at the tree, Thea. And don't worry, I'll be right by your side the entire way." Darren backed away a few steps and changed into the dark wolf of before. Marc, holding her cradled in his arms, stepped into the stream, wading farther and farther until the water tickled her backside, shockingly cold. With Darren's wolf swimming alongside them, Marc, aided by the chilly current, floated and walked them down the hill.

Not a word was spoken. She couldn't, with her teeth chattering from the cold. How he endured immersed halfway she didn't know. Of

Trent and the other wolf, there was no sign.

Did they still follow? Had Roderick's pets caught them?

As twilight gave way to night, she trembled as she wondered how long they had until the vampire himself found them.

I don't want to think about Roderick. Not when escape finally seemed a possibility. She focused instead on the man carrying her. While he didn't inspire the same kind of tingle Darren and Trent had, she still felt something, a little shock more along the lines of that she'd experienced with David. It was totally weird. In the past, her boyfriends had never given her electric shocks when they touched. Could the odd sensation have to do with their wolf status? A weird kind of pheromone thing given how attracted she found herself to the men, despite their deadly situation? Heck, even now, butt half frozen, the cut in her leg throbbing, tense, and stressed, she couldn't deny a certain spurt of heat at being held against his naked chest. A heat that flared higher when she allowed herself to think of Darren or the very naked Trent.

My trauma has made me into a nympho-slut. That or she found herself so happy to have escaped that she welcomed any kind of interaction with another person. Say what you would, talking was nice, but nothing compared to a hug or the intimacy that came from touching almost skin-to-skin. It beat a "Get Well" card any day. *I wonder if there is a card for, "Sorry you got kidnapped by your possessed boyfriend and given over to a psycho vampire who wanted to use your unborn child as a soldier in his army."* Would a card like that come with money in it or the number for the nearest insane asylum?

Except she wasn't crazy. Vampires existed. Or at least one did. And werewolves were all too real and, in some cases, chivalrous and good-looking.

To her surprise they made it downstream without mishap. After staggering out of the chill water, Marc set her on her feet, and she wobbled for a moment as her frozen butt thawed and her cramped legs stretched.

Darren, still in wolf form, slogged from the water and shook, his soaking coat sending droplets flying. She twisted her face and grimaced in his direction.

"I could have done without the wet-dog smell."

She could have sworn his wolf smiled. The man certainly was when he changed shapes, his smooth tanned flesh—so much of it, delineated with well-defined muscles—making her avert her eyes but not before a flicker of heat warmed her belly.

Totally insane.

While Marc scrounged, his arm up to the elbow in a hole at the bottom of a tree, Darren approached her. He crowded her space as he caught her hands in his, warming them with his simple touch.

"How are you holding up?" he asked.

"I'm fine. Shouldn't you be more worried about your friends?"

His lips quirked. "I think they'd be insulted if I wasted my time worrying."

"You guys are weird."

"A good weird I hope?"

"Maybe." The smile that curled her lips with her answer surprised her. How could having this conversation, in the middle of the woods, with a naked stranger, make her happy? She didn't know, but when he answered with a wide grin of his own, her heart pattered faster. *Mine.* Where that possessive thought kept springing from she didn't know, but it also didn't frighten her like it should have. Not when it seemed more and more right.

"Aha. Are you ready to smell like road kill?" Marc asked as he held aloft a couple of bottles filled with cloudy fluids.

He wasn't kidding about the smell. They spritzed her with the vile scent then did themselves. She wondered if it worked by grossing their pursuers out because the stench certainly made her want to run away from herself.

Before she could protest, Darren swung her into his arms.

"Not a word," he warned. "We need to move

fast. And, besides, I like holding you." His startling declaration stunned her. In silence, she clung to him as he ran, wondering if he was perhaps sick. Who enjoyed carrying a pregnant woman in a dirty gown covered in animal pee? Then again, what perverted woman, a captive for weeks in need of a bath, wondered what it would be like to kiss the strong jaw of the profile she couldn't help staring at?

During an attack by three wolves, she was set down for a moment while Darren battled alongside his furry friend. When more howls erupted as soon as they dispatched the trio, Marc tore back in the direction they had come while Darren scooped her up to run again.

She'd given up on arguing with him about it. He seemed bound and determined to rescue her, and, dammit, she was going to let him.

Night had fully fallen by the time they spilled into a parking lot with a single vehicle. He let her down, making sure she had her feet before he dropped to his knees and scrounged under the wheel well. After popping back up, he smiled as he flashed a key at her. In a moment, he'd unlocked the SUV and pulled out not only a jacket to drape over her but a gun as well. He also yanked on a pair of gray track pants but remained shirtless.

"Can you drive?" he asked her as he scanned the forest.

"Why?"

He lifted her into the driver seat. "I want you to get out of here. There's money and a phone in the glove box. Drive as far as you can. When I make it out with my friends, I'll call you."

"You want me to just abandon you?"

He leaned in to start the motor, his arm brushing her lap. She shivered.

"I want you to get to safety. Don't worry about me and the boys. We'll be fine." He pulled away from the door and slammed it shut. He shot her a smile before turning to face the woods.

The temptation to leave, to put the pedal to the floor was strong. She looked at him: he stood straight and tall as he waited for his friends, willing to put his life on the line for her. *For me!* Calling herself all kinds of stupid—*maybe he's a psycho, maybe he's taking me to another vampire*—she rolled down the window.

"I'm not leaving."

He whirled around. "What do you mean you're not leaving? Get out of here while you can."

"Not without you and your friends."

"Don't be stupid. You need to protect yourself and the baby."

A sad smile twisted her lips. "Oddly enough, I think sticking with you and David's brother is probably my best option at this point."

"We will protect you. I will protect you." Intensity imbued his tone, and her breath caught at his gaze.

And as if his declaration had conjured them, four snarling monsters sprang from the forest. To her shock, Darren didn't change shapes. Probably because he would be too vulnerable during the shift. Or so she assumed. He acquitted himself well, but against four, he couldn't prevent the scratches from marring his torso. Staring down at the gun still tucked in her lap, she wavered. *What should I do?* She raised it. She'd never fired one before, but the premise seemed simple. Aim. Pull the trigger.

She'd not counted on the recoil spoiling her shot. Or the deafening noise. With her ears ringing and hand throbbing from where it cracked off the steering wheel, she stared in shock as one of the wolves broke away from the fight with Darren to face her.

With a slow, measured step, snarling and eyes blazing, the beast approached her.

Do something, you idiot. This time when she fired, she used both hands to hold it. The first shot grazed the wolf's side. He yipped and charged. Screaming, she fired again and again until the weapon clicked. Tanned hands plucked the empty weapon from her hands.

"It's okay, honey. You got him," Darren murmured. "It's over. You're safe."

"I—I—" She couldn't manage to squeeze anything out, her throat tight, her eyes burning. *I killed him. It.* It didn't matter. She'd taken a life.

The shock of it rendered her mute. Darren opened the door and leaned in to grab a box from the center console. As he jammed bullets into the chambers, he talked to her in a low, soothing tone.

"It's always hard the first time, honey. That moment when you realize it's you or them. But you did it. You saved yourself. You were so brave."

"I was scared," she whispered.

"Only an idiot wouldn't be," he replied, flipping the chamber back into the gun.

"Do you get scared?"

The grin he flashed her was so mischievous it eased some of her tension. "Honestly? Not much scares me, but then again, I never claimed to be smart."

The crackling of foliage made him whip around, gun pointed. A russet-colored wolf bounded into the clearing followed by the golden and dark-haired one. Their paws no sooner hit the graveled surface than they shifted. Thea averted her eyes. Even with everything she'd been through, staring at a bunch of naked men just seemed wrong.

She crawled into the backseat as it suddenly occurred to her, as they quickly donned pants and shirts, that, given their size, cramming three of them in the back would be a cruel way to repay them for saving her.

Moments later, they piled in, Trent taking the

wheel, while a man of mixed ethnicity took shotgun. Darren climbed in the middle row on one side of her while the redhead claimed the other spot, or tried to. Squeezed tight, the last man in grumbled as Darren shooed him into the back, where he popped up a seat from the floor after shoving some stuff aside.

Tires spun on the loose surface as they sped out of there. For several minutes, silence reigned as Trent drove at a breakneck speed down the winding road leading out of the park. Surrounded by the overly large males, inundated with their presence, Thea shrank in on herself. What previously had seemed like the right thing to do now seemed monumentally stupid.

As if sensing her trepidation, fingers curled around hers, and she glanced sideways to see Darren wearing a soft smile.

"It's okay, honey. Nobody in this truck will hurt you."

"It's in the code," said a voice behind her.

She peeked at the redhead. "What code?"

"The hero code of course. It is our duty to save damsels in distress," he said with broad smile. "At your service, milady." He leaned over the seat to pick up her loose hand and brought it to his lips, brushing a kiss across the top. A tiny tingle went through her, and she didn't protest when he kept her hand enveloped in his.

"Thanks for carrying me."

"My pleasure."

She peered over at the man who'd run with her down the mountain. "I'm sorry. I never properly thanked you. You put your life on the line for me. You all did."

"No thanks needed, honey. I'd do it again in a heartbeat." She returned Darren's soft smile, at ease with him, yet not understanding why. When he tugged her closer to him, she didn't protest, the warmth of his body welcome, dispelling the chill in hers.

"I'm Jaxon by the way," the beautiful cocoa skinned man offered from the front. "And the grim one driving is Trent."

Trent grunted instead of replying.

"We met already. He's David's brother."

"Excellent," the one called Jaxon said. "So, now that we're no longer strangers, care to tell us what happened?"

"I—I—" The words to her story stuck in her throat as the enormity of it all came crashing in on her. The hands holding hers tightened.

"It's okay, honey. Take your time."

"Fuck that. I want to know what happened to my brother," Trent bit out.

His brusque tone sparked her anger, especially considering who he was asking about. "I told you. David's dead." She didn't add *good riddance*, but her tone implied it.

"I know you did, but you also said he killed himself."

"Yup." She didn't elucidate any further.

"How?"

"Claw across the throat." She turned her face into Darren's arm as the memory of it flashed through her mind.

Trent slammed the steering wheel. "Fuck! How could this have happened? He must have been really desperate to do that. I'll bet it's those rogues' fault. I want to know why those bastards have been allowed to fester in those mountains, preying on other wolves like my brother."

"Stop talking like he was a victim. Your brother was one of them. He knew what he was doing. Who he was hurting." Her flat answer saw the SUV swerving as Trent craned to glare at her.

"Like fuck. David would never belong to a group of psychos like that, and he wouldn't hurt a fly."

"Sorry to break it to you, but he did. He's the one who went crazy all of a sudden. Who killed my neighbor then hit me and took me to that place. Who gave me to that fucking monster. He's the one who didn't lift a finger to save me or our child and then took the cowardly way out by killing himself."

"You're lying!"

"I wish."

"Leave her alone," Darren growled. "You asked for answers. She's given you some. If you don't like them, too fucking bad. Or have you forgotten that you didn't know David as well as you thought? He lied to you for what, three, four months?"

"There's got to be a reason," Trent muttered, taking a sharp turn that saw them skidding onto the main road. The momentum shoved her into Darren, who let go of her hand to tuck her under his arm.

"The reason is Roderick," Jaxon supplied. "I told you that vampire could command wolves."

"You know him?" she asked as she faced forward, surprised they knew of the monster.

"We've met, yes. It didn't work out so well for me," Jaxon replied. With him turned to speak to her, she saw the sadness on his face.

"But you escaped him? It's possible then. He told me I could never hope to be free. That I could run as far as I wanted but he'd always find me."

"That is probably the only true thing that vampire has ever said," Jaxon replied.

"Don't listen to him," Marc interrupted. "Now that we've got you, we aren't letting anyone get you back. Even pointy-toothed undead things that aren't supposed to exist."

She slumped. "I'm screwed."

"Why would you say that? I already told you I would protect you, and Marc's also volunteered. Once Trent gets over his snit, I'm sure he's going to want to help out, too."

A bitter chuckle emerged from Jaxon. "But she's right. She is screwed. Unless you can get her into the safety of a pack, you won't be enough to stand against him. Even then, a pack might have a hard time keeping her from his clutches if he's really determined."

"We won't get any help from the pack. Nathan, our temporary alpha, declared us rogue for leaving," Trent said, showing that, despite his anger and focus on the road, he'd paid attention to the conversation.

"Call him up and tell him we've changed our mind," Marc answered. "You found the answer you were looking for, so there's no reason to stay away anymore."

Jaxon shook his head. "Once they learn you've come in contact with the vampire, they will probably shoot the lot of you on sight. Nathan and the rest of the council have learned that only those with the strongest minds can resist Roderick's compulsions. And because he can hide his tainting presence so well, they won't trust any of you. Even the girl."

Trent's gravelly tone slid into the conversation. "Then I guess there's only one solution. We need to kill the vampire."

Why did she get the impression the expression "easier said than done" applied in this case?

Jaxon laughed, a derisive sound. "Oh, yes. Because we've not tried that one before. Holy water? Yeah, that's only for the movies. Bullets, even to the head? Brings him down for only moments. I've yet to get close enough for a decapitation or wooden stake, and flame throwers are hard to find."

"There has to be a way or the world would be overrun with the fanged fuckers," Trent growled.

"Why don't we ask another vampire?" Marc added.

Several pairs of eyes turned to regard him. He shrugged. "You can't tell me that a society that's managed to keep itself secret for thousands of years, other than the occasional bad flick, is going to be happy about one of their kind running around killing people, pissing off wolves, and kidnapping pregnant women. Hell, wolves are a violent, not easily controlled group, and we still managed to create laws and enforce them."

Darren's answer emerged thoughtful and slow. "He has a point. Someone created him. So there must be someone who knows how to unmake him."

"But how do we find them?"

That was a question no one possessed an answer to.

Chapter Six

Finding a motel several hours later proved easy. Getting rid of the emotions churning in his mind, not so much. When Trent had embarked on his quest to find his brother, he'd never expected it would end in tragedy. How could David be dead? How could he have turned from the shy and gentle teen Trent knew into a man capable of violence toward a woman and, if she could be believed—and his gut said she could—worse? As if that weren't hard enough to swallow, he'd apparently killed himself. What horror had his little brother endured to take such a cowardly route? Trent needed to know more, which meant talking to the woman his brother had impregnated, mated with, and hurt. Knowing the next step didn't stop him from stalling.

Thea scared him. Not scared in an I'm-afraid-she's-going-to-kick-my-ass way, but in a why-do-I-think-she's-hotter-than-hell way, which seemed totally inappropriate for a lot of reasons. For one, in spite of the battle, the danger, and the mission, as well as her refugee appearance, he took one look at her and wanted her. Wanted her fucking badly—naked, skin-to-skin.

So fucking wrong. As a victim of abuse, she deserved compassion and caring, not lusty thoughts. But knowing this didn't stop him from imagining it, his tongue sliding across her creamy skin while his cock was buried balls-deep in her and her nails raked his back. He tried to focus on a different kind of hunger since it had been hours since he'd eaten. What did he picture? Not a medium-rare burger. Oh, no. He saw himself with his face between her thighs, licking her cream. Her on her knees peering up at him with her lips stretched around his dick, bobbing and sucking.

No two ways about it: he wanted her in his bed. Or on the floor. Wall. Actually anywhere he could get a few minutes of privacy and get rid of the ache in his shaft. It made no sense.

As if his inexplicable arousal wasn't bad enough, she carried a babe in her belly. She was pregnant with his brother's kid. And there was the slight snag of the mating mark on her neck that he'd seen, which he'd wager also belonged to David. Just freaking great. It wasn't bad enough he had all this other shit to deal with. Now he wanted to claim his brother's bloody widow.

Someone shoot because I've obviously gone insane.

A smart man would stay away from the girl, but then again, he'd never gotten good grades in anything. And besides, he wasn't sure if he could stand aside, not with his wolf chafing to get closer or with his jealousy burning and demanding action as he saw the interest his friends showed in her.

Was she meant to be their mate? Did their wolves howl to join with her like his did? Could he settle down with a woman who'd bedded his brother first? Actually, that was the least of his problems. In his world, brothers often shared the same woman because it was easiest.

Humans would be appalled that Lycans engaged in polyamorous relationships. Up to four men per woman. It had always been that way, and while the shifter council was slowly coming around to changing those laws, Trent didn't see the packs adapting as quickly, not when females of their kind were so rare.

Females of their kind?

Stunned at a sudden insight, Trent got out of the truck and strode to the motel door. He didn't knock before entering and ended up facing off against Darren and Marc. Jaxon never budged from his chair, although he did have his gun pointed at the doorway.

"Holy fuck, Trent. Knock next time, would you? I could have blown your head off." Jaxon lowered his weapon.

"Where is she?" Trent asked when he didn't spot her.

"Taking a shower. Why?" Darren asked.

"She can't be pregnant with David's kid," he blurted out.

"What are you talking about? Are you saying she's a liar?" Marc replied, arching a brow.

"Or are you calling her a slut?" Darren

growled.

"Neither, but face facts. We've all smelled her." Nods all around. "She smells human. We can't impregnate humans."

His words sank in, but Jaxon shook his head. "Wrong. Kind of. Yes, we can't impregnate humans. But we discovered something interesting about dormants. If they're mated to a true mate, sometimes their wolf can come forth."

"Bullshit. I've never heard of it."

Jaxon shrugged. "The knowledge is only recent and is not widely known. We found out with my mate, Bailey, it was possible. She was human when we met her. After we rescued her from Roderick's clutches, we noticed something different about her, not quite wolfish but not a hundred percent human. On the full moon, after Gavin mated with and bedded her, she shifted. It wasn't pretty."

"So he woke her wolf? And then she got pregnant?"

Jaxon nodded.

"But Thea is pregnant, and she still smells human."

"What would you like me to say? As I mentioned, this is new territory for all of us. I know Nathan's got some pack doctors working on the dilemma because, in case it hadn't occurred to you, how many dormants have left the packs over the years? How many of them are in the general human population, oblivious to their possible heritage? How many of us have not met our true mate because we didn't look to those shunned for being considered unsound?"

Marc whistled. "Which means how many have woken up, not knowing what's happening and not knowing how to find their way back to the pack?"

"Those latent wolves aren't our problem," Darren interjected. "But Thea is. She smells human, no doubt about that, but despite that, my wolf is fucking spinning. I've never had this kind of reaction to a woman before. I know she's gone through a trauma, but I'm stating right now, I intend to court her."

"I guess we'll be taking turns," Marc added with a laugh. "What about you, Trent?"

Trent clamped his jaw before he also threw his hat into the ring. He wasn't ready to concede anything. "She's my brother's widow. And a victim of abuse. I'd say it's too early for anybody to be thinking of claiming her as mate. While all your declarations are noble, I still don't see how a human can be pregnant with a wolf's pup. We've had dormants mated with wolves before and not seen any progeny."

"There is that fact," Jaxon agreed. "But Thea and Bailey have one thing in common. Roderick. In both cases, the girls were victims in his care. Who knows what he did to them to make their wolf emerge. Perhaps he's the key in all this. If we go with that assumption, then let's say

Roderick finds the girl and recognizes her somehow as latent. He knows from his experiment with Bailey that a mating bond is needed to fully wake the beast. Instead of immediately kidnapping her, probably because he had his hands full fighting me and the packs off, he leaves her be but starts sending some of his minions her way. David in this case. She and David hit it off. Maybe her dormant wolf recognizes David as her mate. They hook up, Roderick does some of his vampire mojo, and her wolf wakes but, for some reason, doesn't fully emerge. Yet. But she changes enough that your brother can impregnate her."

"That's a lot of what-ifs," Trent muttered.

"Got another explanation?"

Marc turned pensive. "So, if your theory is correct, she could turn furry on a full moon?"

"Doubtful until she's carried the baby to term."

Jaxon laughed. "Who's volunteering to explain that one to her? Hey, Thea, by the way, we think the vampire might have experimented on you so you could turn into a wolf, but don't worry, that probably won't happen until after you birth a puppy."

"This isn't funny," Trent growled.

"No, but you have to admit, the conversation is going to be interesting."

"Do we have to tell her right away?" Darren asked. "Why don't we wait and let her get used to us first? I'm sure she'll have a lot of questions about our kind. We can reassure her that we're not that scary before springing the news."

"We don't have time to mollycoddle her. She still needs to give us more answers on what happened." Because, *dammit*, Trent wanted to find a way to deny what his brother seemed to have done and at least have him die with dignity. A more selfish part of him wanted to be wrong about his apparent mating to Thea. "How long has she been in there?"

Several sets of eyes turned toward the one closed door, and Trent heard the gurgle of water.

"Can you wait to question her until after she's had a chance to bathe? It's the least we can give her after what she suffered." Darren gave Trent a challenging stare; however, Trent wasn't about to drag a pregnant woman out of a well-deserved shower. Join her maybe, but that was a whole different scenario.

"While she's out of hearing, should we discuss what we are going to do next?" Marc asked.

Do next? How about stripping and getting into the shower with her? Trent's mind filled with an image of Thea, a wet and naked Thea.

"Stop drooling, man. Weren't you the one who said we needed to take it slow?"

Slapped with his own rebuke, Trent scowled. "I don't know what to do next. It's not like there's a help book when it comes to dealing with vampires and their minions. Or an 800 number we can call. I'd welcome any suggestions."

Silence greeted him.

"I think what we all need is a good night's rest," Jaxon announced. "I'd recommend keeping someone on watch, though, just in case those wolfies managed to track us. We'll regroup in the morning once our heads are clearer."

Somehow Trent didn't think the churning in his mind would disappear by morning. And looking at his friends, staring at the closed bathroom door, he'd bet they battled the same dilemma.

* * * *

Thea hid like a coward in the bathroom. She'd jumped on the chance for a shower, locking the door behind her and stripping the stinking gown from her body. Oh, to feel clean again. She cranked the water until steam rose before she stepped in. The hot spray hit the gash on her thigh, and she hissed. In the mad flight down the mountain then the wild race to get away, she'd actually forgotten about it. Peeking down at it, she noted it didn't seem as ragged as before, the edges sealed together, healing already, impossible as it seemed.

Turning her attention away from the cut, she tilted her face into the spray to let its cleansing warmth wash the traces of her captivity from her skin. The tiny shampoo bottle that all motels seemed to stock gave enough to soap and rinse twice. As for the bar of soap, she scrubbed herself almost raw with it to erase the taint of her captors and scrub the vile remembered touches from her skin until she shone more red than healthy pink.

With nothing left to wash, she leaned her forehead on the tile and just let the water cascade down her bare shoulders. Let herself finally think.

What am I going to do?

Hours ago, she'd waited to die, but her unexpected rescue meant she had a second chance. *We have a second chance.* She cupped her rounded abdomen. But a chance to do what? And go where? Roderick wouldn't let her go without a fight. He'd have a hard time finding them tonight—or so she hoped. However, he would track her, find her, and when he did . . .

Will I be alone, unable to defend myself, or among men who've proven themselves capable of fighting? Or at least they were skilled at fighting wolves like themselves. How they would fare against the vampire remained unknown. Chances were they'd cave to Roderick's will like David and the others had, doing his bidding, which meant she was screwed.

Screwed if I stay. Screwed if I leave. The water turned cold, matching the chill that clutched her heart as despair, her close friend, returned.

She turned off the tap and sank to the bottom of the tub, the noisy fan in the ceiling muffling her sobs. She was so tired of being scared. So tired of...

A scream left her lips as the door to the bathroom smashed open and bodies crowded outside the curtain then tore it open. With only a heartbeat to scramble, she pulled her knees up and together in front of her bulging belly, draping her arms over the top as she tried to cover herself from the gaze of three pairs of eyes turned her way.

"What's wrong?"

"Do you need help?"

"For Christ's sake, someone hand her a towel."

The overlapping inquiries and demands stopped her sobs, but her breathing still hitched as she stared at them, her cheeks damp with tears.

Darren knelt at the side of the tub and draped a towel over her shoulders, the corner of it hitting her legs. She clutched it and shivered.

"Why are you all in here?" she stammered when they continued to watch with grim expressions.

"We heard you crying and thought you were in trouble."

Heard her? His simple claim slapped her with the fact that these men, no matter how nice they seemed, were not human. They were animals. Animals like David and the others who'd hurt her. Terror gripped her, and her tears flooded anew. *What do they want from me?*

"Shh, honey. You're safe now." Darren reached a hand out to stroke her cheek. She flinched, her head tilting back to escape his gentle touch. "I'm sorry," he whispered, chagrin thick in his voice. "I wasn't thinking."

"The girl's fine. Just overwrought from her experience," Trent snapped. "Sorry we barged in. There's a clean T-shirt on the vanity and some track pants. They won't fit too good, but it's the best we can do for the moment." The man with the face of her old lover turned on his heel and stalked out.

The red-haired one, Marc, gave her a sad smile. "Don't cry. Darren's right when he says you're safe now. We won't let anyone hurt you." He left.

"I'm sorry I'm such a wimp," she whispered.

"I'd say you've done pretty good. You escaped, didn't you?"

"With help. I'd given up, you know. Thought I was going to die in that room."

"But you didn't. And when the chance arose, you took it and escaped. There's no shame in accepting help. I'm just glad we found you."

"So am I. What happens now?"

"What do you want to do? I don't think returning to your old home is the best idea, though."

"God, no. He'd find me too easily." *But where can I go?*

"Don't worry. We'll find somewhere safe for you."

She wished she could believe that. A shiver went through her.

"Damn. I'm sorry. Here I am yakking at you while you're wet and freezing. I'll bet you're hungry, too. I'll get out of here and get us some food while you get dressed. And we promise not to barge in unless we hear screaming next time. Sorry if we scared you. That wasn't our intention."

Before she could tell Darren he didn't frighten her, he left the splintered door closed, not snugly but enough to give her some privacy. She could do nothing, however, about the confusion in her mind because, despite her fear, despite worrying about what they wanted from her, she found herself drawn to him. And Trent, despite his crude exterior. Even Marc drew her, to a certain extent. She also wanted to trust them.

I'm sick. Or suffering from some kind of syndrome. Didn't they have a name for victims who thought themselves attracted to their rescuers? Whatever they called it, she had it, bad, but it didn't mean she'd do anything about it. Now wasn't the time to worry about why very different-seeming men attracted her and had fooled her into thinking she could rely on them. More important things, such as keeping her and the baby safe, needed to take precedence over everything else.

As she rose, she wrapped the towel under her armpits and secured it between her breasts before she stepped out. Her fear receded with their willingness to give her space and privacy. It didn't mean she trusted them or wanted them touching her, but it allowed her to push back her terror enough to function. She dressed in the clothes Trent had left, his by the scent: a worn black T-shirt with Jimi Hendrix on the front and track pants. She pulled the drawstring as tight as she could and rolled the cuffs. They'd not brought anything for her feet, but she did notice a comb and a toothbrush still in its wrapper. She made use of them while staring at herself in the mirror.

I look the same. Oh, a little bit paler, her cheeks not as rounded, but the marks of her ordeal, the trauma, none of it showed on her face. Other than the long scratch on her leg, she'd bear no lasting scars unless she counted the ones on her psyche. But even those were fading. She'd learned after the death of her parents that dwelling on the past accomplished nothing. Living in a world of pity changed nothing. What had happened to her sucked. It would always suck. And she'd have nightmares and probably some panic attacks, but life went on. She would go on.

Or at least until Roderick got his claws on her

again. And now she noticed a change in the mirror, especially in her eyes, where fear shone, a beacon for the monster.

* * * *

While Darren left to get some food with Trent, Marc paced the room, his usually carefree mind in turmoil.

With a leg thrown over the arm of a chair, Jaxon watched. "Something on your mind?"

"The girl." Marc hesitated and looked at the bathroom door. It remained shut, the fan still whirring loudly. "She's scared of me. Of all of us."

"Can you blame her?"

"No, but I don't want her to be." Marc, the most benign of his kind, was always willing to give a lady a hand and crack a smile. But now his pride had been struck low by a woman. It sucked.

"I'm afraid there's not much any of us can do about that. The girl's been through a trauma. It will take time and understanding before she heals. And it won't be easy, given you're going to have to run to keep her safe."

"Aren't you being a tad paranoid? We're hours from his lair. There's no tracks leading to us. What makes you think this vampire fellow will follow?"

"Oh, he'll come," Jaxon promised. "And

when he does, he's going to try and control you. You might not even realize it's happening. You'll think you've escaped his clutches. You'll live and laugh and love. Then, wham, when you least expect it, the bastard will be pulling your strings and you'll be dancing to his tune, whether you like it or not. Betraying those you love."

"Just because it happened to you doesn't mean it will happen to me."

A shrug lifted Jaxon's shoulders. "If you want to live in that fantasy world, go ahead. But no crying later when I say I told you so."

"So what do you think we should do?"

"If Thea were Bailey, and I were in your shoes, I'd beg for the pack to take her in and keep a close eye on her. Then I'd go find myself some vampires and get on my knees and ask them to help me take down Roderick."

"Why haven't you done that?"

"Who says I haven't? I've been looking while tracking the undead fucker. But it's not like I can post an ad saying 'Hey, vampire dudes, lonely werewolf looking for tips on killing your kind.'"

"There must be a way to contact them. How did the old council get in touch and make the trade with Roderick? They obviously knew how to talk to the fangers."

"Yeah, but they wouldn't give Nathan and the others the information, even when sentenced for crimes against the pack."

"So we need to get their attention," Marc

said, an idea forming in his mind. "We theorized earlier in the truck that they probably aren't crazy about Roderick drawing all this attention to himself. So we should use that to our advantage. What if we made their existence really public? In-your-face impossible to ignore."

"I take it you have a plan?"

"The beginnings of one at any rate."

"That's better than we've got so far."

Which was squat. Energized, Marc paced quicker, letting the idea ferment. "I want to run it by the other guys first, but if this Roderick is as hard to kill as you claim, then we need to do it."

The door to the bathroom creaked, and Marc whirled. Cautious eyes regarded him.

"Where is everyone?"

"Gone to get food. Are you hungry?" He spoke softly.

She nodded before opening the door wider and stepping out. His wolf whined at the fear it scented coming off her in waves. Peeking about, she appeared like prey, skittish and ready to bolt at the slightest motion.

Something about her intrigued him and his beast. It wasn't the lightning bolt he'd expected when others talked of their true mate, but he definitely found himself attracted. And horny. Very horny, even if she looked like a refugee dressed in oversized clothing. But his arousal wasn't something he could act on—yet. Marc gestured to the TV. "Did you want me to turn it on? It's got cable." Yeah, that was suave. He wanted to slap himself.

A shake of her head answered him. She came farther into the room and perched on the foot of the bed closest to her.

A need to sit beside her and envelop her in his arms shook him to the core. Something about Thea brought out every protective instinct he owned. Plus some. She called to him, even in her fragile state, he who usually liked his woman as loud and ribald as him.

Jaxon made a noise. "Jeez, people, it's not a fucking funeral. We escaped. Intact. There will be time later on to walk on eggshells."

"Shut up," Marc hissed. "You'll scare her."

A sound escaped her, and he whirled, ready to apologize for Jaxon's rude outburst. He found her stifling a smile.

"He's right, you know. You don't have to tiptoe. I'll admit the situation kind of has me wigged, but I'll get over it."

"Ah, but I was looking forward to having a reason to hit him."

Now she did smile. "Don't let me stop you."

"Hey!" Jaxon exclaimed. "Is that any way to thank the guy who provided the diversion to rescue your ass?"

She sobered immediately, and Marc almost did smack him. "No, it's not. I forgot to say thank you. And you," she said, raising her gaze to his. "I never thought I'd escape. It was very brave what you did."

An urge to scuff his feet, blush, and mutter, "Aw shucks," struck Marc. He found his balls instead. "No problem. Are you thirsty? We grabbed some pop, water, and juice from the vending machine."

"Apple?"

"I've got two." He tossed her the bottle unthinkingly then gaped in horror as it soared at her. She snatched it out of the air.

A grin tilted her lips. "I might not be athletic, but I still remember how to catch things. My dad wanted a boy. He got me instead, so he adapted. Tossing a baseball around, following football, and climbing trees are just a few of the things he taught me."

The reference to her father made him curse. "Shit, your parents. Did you want to call them and let them know you're safe?"

A shadow crossed her face. "My parents died years ago. I have no one to call."

"I'm sorry."

She shrugged. "It happens."

"In the pack, no one is ever alone. We live as a community and help each other."

"The pack? You mean there are more people like you?"

"People like us are called Lycans," Jaxon drawled. "And you might want to think about dropping the look of distaste, darling, because, if I'm right, you're also a wolf."

That statement saw her spitting out a mouthful of juice. "Like fuck!" She slapped a hand over her mouth, and her eyes rounded in astonishment.

Marc couldn't help himself. He laughed and was still laughing when Trent walked in with Darren and several paper bags smelling of fast food.

"What's so funny?"

"Our pregnant mama over there has a potty mouth."

"I do not," she exclaimed, her cheeks sporting bright red spots. "It just slipped out because of what Jaxon said."

"What did he say?" Darren asked as he pulled stuff out of the bags and laid it atop the scarred dresser at the foot of the beds.

"He says I'm a wolf thing like you. But I'm not. I've never been bitten or anything, and I don't get an urge to howl at the moon."

Jaxon snickered. "You forgot to add scratching behind your ears and chasing cars."

She planted her hands on her hips. She looked too cute with her oversized T-shirt, damp hair curling around her head, and loose pants rolled into thick cuffs at the bottom. "You can stop making fun of me. Grateful for your rescue doesn't mean I'm going to let you brainwash me into thinking I'm something that I'm not."

"Whatever you say, darling."

"Ignore him," Darren said, blocking her view

of Jaxon. He handed her a burger and carton of fries. "Eat. You need to keep your strength up, for you and the baby."

She took the food and sat, but she gazed up at Darren, her white teeth chewing worriedly at her lower lip. "Do you think I'm a wolf?"

"The possibility of your being a Lycan has come up. I can't say for certain, though, whether you are or not. Honestly, we probably won't know for sure until you birth your child and the first full moon comes around."

"Pregnancy stops it?"

"In most cases. We think its nature's way of protecting the baby from the violence of the shift."

"What do you think? Am I?"

Darren took a deep breath, and Marc found himself taking one too, sifting her scent, letting it wash over his senses. His wolf growled. *Pack*.

Darren answered her question, brave man. Marc didn't want to become the bearer of bad news. "I think that your body is changing, waking from its dormant state."

"But what if I don't want to be a wolf? How do I stop it from happening after the baby is born? I can't stay pregnant forever."

Flopping on the bed beside the one she perched on, Marc reached over and snagged a fry, startling her. "Oh, it's not that bad. So you'll turn furry once a month. You'll also be stronger, faster, and more resilient."

"Hairy, fanged, and scary," she retorted.

"And if you get caught in the rain, your whole house will smell like wet dog," Trent added. "Get over it. You can't change it, so either embrace it or learn to live with it."

"You're nothing like your brother," she stated baldly.

A dead silence descended. Her eyes narrowed thoughtfully as Trent went still.

His alpha and friend took a swig of pop before answering. "Why, because I won't lie to you and tell you what you want to hear?"

"No, because you have the guts to speak your mind. Your brother was more . . . ." She paused.

"Wishy-washy," Trent supplied, his frank appraisal not a shock to Marc, who'd known David—and would have picked on him had he not been his friend's younger sibling.

She looked pensive. "Yes. When I first met him, he was one of those really nice guys. If you asked does my ass look fat in this, he'd say it looks awesome. You, though," she said as she looked right at Trent, "would tell me it looked huge, I'll bet."

He grinned. "Yup, but just so we're clear, I like big butts."

"And I cannot lie," Jaxon sang.

Darren groaned. "No. Not that stupid song again."

A chuckle slipped from Marc at her questioning look. "The song plays a lot on the radio stations out here, and our new friend Jaxon loves to sing along."

"I've walked into the *Twilight Zone*," she exclaimed, but she smiled as she said it. As if they'd practiced, all of them broke out humming the theme song of popular TV show that lived on through the Internet and DVDs.

Even better than the moment of companionship was the fact that she no longer emitted the frightened scent. Nor did she slap Marc's hand when he kept stealing her fries. Things were already looking up.

* * * *

Thea let the conversation flow over her as she ate the burger—two of them—and fries. Hungry and more at ease, she didn't talk much, but she did listen avidly. After the *Twilight Zone* remark, they discussed for several minutes the shows of the past they missed most. A closet *Bewitched* fan, Marc sheepishly admitted he'd crushed on Samantha large when younger, whereas Darren, with a grin, said it was Mary Ann from *Gilligan's Island* with her pigtails. As for Trent, he ate in silence, but his gaze seemed to fixate on her, although when she dared meet it, he looked away. Before long, a tickling sensation would let her know he watched again.

He unnerved her. Not because of his resemblance to David or the fact that he seemed angry at her, the world, and everything in general—all good reasons to stay clear—but the thing that surprised her most was how attracted she was to him. Him and Darren actually. Marc, unfortunately, while kind and good-looking, only inspired a weak warmth. Trent and Darren, though... Just looking at them had her tummy doing somersaults and warmth flooding her.

Having just escaped Hell, she should have been a huddled ball of misery. Instead, she wanted to dance and rejoice. She should have sworn a pledge to stay away from all men, wolves in particular, considering her own recent experience. However, she couldn't deny a certain womanly pleasure when Darren smiled at her. Or the fascination with Trent's hard body, hidden now but still so vivid in her mind.

Maybe it's the pregnancy hormones making me horny. Still, there was horny and then there was lusting after two guys. A reverse *Big Love*, a TV show she'd watched with fascination. How did the women handle their jealousies when it came to sharing? Thea could never share a man. Couldn't stand the thought that another woman had touched and caressed the same skin. What she'd always wondered, but the show seemed to deny, was if in those polygamous relationships, things ever went beyond one-on-one. Did the guy ever take two or three of his wives to bed at once? Logically, unless he'd taken some Viagra, he could find completion with only one. *Whereas a woman with multiple male lovers could technically please several at once.*

She blinked, stunned at how her mind had gone into that wacky direction. *Did they spike my burger with something?* Watching them converse, more or less ignoring her except for occasional glances, she held back a sigh. As if they were overcome with lust for a pregnant refugee.

Keeping that thought in mind, she stuffed her face with more fries and tuned back in to the conversation. There seemed to be a debate going on about which direction they should go next.

She didn't really care so long as it was far, far away. However, if they were to be believed, distance wouldn't let her escape the seemingly impossible fact that she was a wolf. *Yeah, right.* She didn't want to believe them. The fact of the matter was, though, she'd noticed something different about herself. Subtle things, like her rapid healing, her sharpened eyesight, keener hearing, oh, and super hairy legs.

As she cupped her belly she began to wonder if the baby was going to be a wolf, too. As if sensing her thoughts, Darren, who'd scooped a seat beside her, placed his hand over hers.

"How far along?"

"Four or five months. I don't know for sure. I was supposed to go see my doctor the week after my kidnapping, and I'm still not quite sure how long he held me captive for."

"Next town we'll hit a clinic and get you and

the baby checked out."

"Is that safe?"

"It should be. Roderick would have a hard time infiltrating all the medical practices."

"No, I mean, if David was a wolf and I might be, won't the baby . . ." She trailed off.

He grinned. "If you're worried there's a litter of puppies in there, then relax. We don't shift until puberty, and short of an extravagant DNA test, it doesn't show up as anything obvious on blood samples."

"Oh good to know." A large yawn saw her blushing in embarrassment. "Sorry. I guess I'm more tired than I thought." She should have been comatose, actually, given they'd escaped the previous afternoon and driven most of the night. Dawn had already come and gone at this point. No wonder her eyes blinked in fatigue.

"The adrenaline has worn off, and your belly is full. It's time all of us went to sleep."

Sleep? Eyeing the four men and two queen-sized beds, she wondered at the plan.

Darren chuckled. "It's okay, honey. You don't need to worry about us hogging the bed. Two of us will share the bed beside you while the other pair keeps watch for trouble."

"Oh. Thanks." Surely she wasn't disappointed she was going to sleep alone?

A soft smile curved his lips. "My pleasure." He hopped off the bed and pulled back the sheets before motioning for her to climb in. She did, her eyes shutting as soon as her head hit the pillow. He draped the covers over her and whispered, "Good night," a chorus echoed by the others, sending her off to sleep.

Chapter Seven

A sense of something wrong made Trent fidget on the rooftop where he hid for this second round of watch. He'd opted to stand his guard duty outside for this shift while Jaxon covered the inside. Darren and Marc slept, their turn for guard duty not for another hour still. They needed the sleep after the grueling trek of the day before. Night had completely fallen, yet the thick cloud cover hid the stars, rendering the world dark and damp.

At least out here in the brisk fall air Trent could breathe deep and not taste her scent. Not hunger for *her*. After her shower, it was all he could do to keep his hands off her. To prevent himself from snarling at the others for daring to show an interest. Trent was not a jealous man by nature. How could he be while raised in a pack where polyamorous situations were the accepted norm? But knowing Thea was available, if a widow, with others circling her in interest, he couldn't help the possessive feeling. The need to claim her as his own.

Utter fucking madness.

To keep himself from doing or saying something stupid, he took first watch and headed outside. How he'd managed to sleep when his turn came, in the same room as her, smelling her so close, he didn't know. What made her so irresistible? A stranger to him and his kind, why would his wolf think she was their mate? Could the fact that she carried a pup, related to him by blood, confuse his beast? But no, an urge to protect was a far cry from what he wanted, which was to strip her naked and caress every inch of her no matter how wrong—but pleasurable.

Lost in his chaotic thoughts, he almost missed the motion below. Snapping to attention, he stayed low, crouched amidst the chimneys and stacks on the roof, focused on the parking lot. Downwind of him, and hugging the parked vehicles, shadows moved in his direction, toward the room they'd rented the previous night. Against all odds, the rogues found them.

As per their plan, he let his foot knock once on the rooftop, knowing Jaxon would hear it and wake the others. Unfortunately, the slight sound, louder than he would have wished in the silent night, made the approaching rogues pause. Not wanting to risk premature discovery, not when he still might have the element of surprise on his side, Trent didn't move, didn't breathe as he waited to see what they would do. *Come on, you bastards. Just a little closer.* Close enough that he could swoop upon them like a furry angel of death.

However, the rogues decided against further stealth. As if possessed of one mind, they howled, a loud ululation sure to make any humans listening piss themselves in fear. Trent cursed as he realized, despite the nearly dozen wolves they'd dispatched earlier, there was probably another two dozen ready and willing to battle.

Fight or flee. Trent leaned toward the former; however, he didn't just have himself to consider.

Fuck.

Swinging down off the roof, he hit the pavement just as the door opened. Jaxon leapt out, followed by Marc, while Darren hovered in the doorframe. Thea's frightened eyes peered out from behind him.

"Get her in the truck. We need to get out of here." Easier said than done when three shapes came hurtling over said vehicle. Marc, a chair leg in one hand, Jaxon, his revolver pointed, and Trent, hands half shifted in a feat only strong alphas could accomplish, met their charge.

Bloodlust immediately coursed through his body as he ripped and tore through the fur-covered skin. He dispatched the first attacker in time for the second lunging one. Then a third. By the time he danced with a fourth, while still trying to put down the previous two, Darren was in the truck with Thea cowering beside him.

The engine roared to life, the headlights lighting up the darkness, reflecting off dozens of eyes pinpricked in red.

"Holy fuck!"

Trent could only silently agree with Marc's exclamation. Forget fighting. With those kinds of numbers it would end up a massacre.

"Drive!" he screamed to Darren. They didn't have time to dispatch the wolves closest to them and climb in before the rest descended on them. But Trent had a plan, and if luck was on his side, it would work.

Darren shot the truck into reverse; its heavy frame, reinforced with steel on the bumpers, hit a few bodies and sent them flying. His pack brother then slammed the vehicle forward, aiming right at Trent and Marc, while Jaxon, laughing like a maniac, ran off to the left as he fired his gun.

The wolves, busy trying to tear his and Marc's throats out, didn't even flinch as the truck barreled at them. Trent didn't share the same death wish, and he dove out of the way just in time. The truck impacted his opponents with a thump that sent the rogues flying. Trent vaulted up, grabbing hold of the roof rails. Marc landed alongside him and flipped himself up. He scrambled to the front. And Trent joined him on the hard top then held on. Darren, cursing up a streak as he slammed on the gas again, hit the sidewalk. The SUV went up on two wheels as he turned sharply. The truck thumped hard when it landed, knocking Trent's teeth together. Not the most elegant of maneuvers, but it got them going in the right direction.

With a squeal of tires, Darren sped away, weaving through the parked vehicles toward a lone figure surrounded by furry bodies. That crazy bastard Jaxon was still laughing, his face more a rictus of pain than mirth as he fired at the never-ending wave. As Darren plowed the truck through the snarling mass, Trent leaned over and held out a hand. Thankfully, Jaxon caught it, and he swung up on the roof behind him.

Lights switched on in the various motel units as the cacophony of the attack woke the human patrons. Trent didn't worry about being recognized. The sight of three men riding atop an SUV probably paled in comparison to the number of wolves snarling in the parking lot.

Driving like a man possessed with a need for speed, Darren careened onto the main road and really poured on the gas. Wind whipping through his hair, holding on for dear life lest he fall off and suffer a major case of road rash, Trent couldn't help but laugh when Marc whooped.

"Shiiiit! Now that's what I call a getaway."

And while it seemed a clean one, one crucial fact remained, Trent thought as he listened to the howling behind them. The rogues had located them once against all odds, which meant they could find them again.

At a red light, Darren slowed down, less for the possible cops than for a chance for Trent and the others to clamber into the truck. Trent found himself in the backseat with Thea beside him.

Shaking like a leaf, she hugged herself, and a wave of compassion flowed over him.

Without thinking twice, he tugged her against him. She resisted at first, but against his strength, she couldn't escape. Arm wrapped around her, he didn't say a word, just let her soak in some of his warmth and strength. Slowly, the tension in her body eased.

"Better now?" he asked quietly, more to not startle her because, surrounded by Lycans, short of mentally projecting his words, he couldn't speak low enough for them not to hear.

"I guess. That was pretty scary. How did they find us?"

"I don't know." He hated admitting that because it made her tense up.

"It's because Roderick has a link to someone in this truck," Jaxon stated quietly.

"I'm sorry," she whispered.

"For what? Just because you were his prisoner doesn't make you the automatic suspect," Jaxon said. "For all I know my bond with the devil works two ways and he can sense me, too. Or he managed to snag a hook in one of your suitors."

"No one's controlling me," Trent growled.

"So you think," Jaxon replied with an enigmatic smile.

Marc craned around in his seat. "How would we know who's the culprit? Is there some kind of test we can do? Shine a flashlight in our eyes and look for red spots or something?"

"Or eat some garlic while standing in sunlight?" Darren retorted. "I can't believe the paranoia coming out of all of you. Did it ever occur to you to look for the logical explanation?"

Trent frowned. Why had he assumed so quickly that Jaxon's theory was the correct one? He didn't believe in mind-controlling vampires. Sick rogues, yes. Vampires who could make people dance like kites on a string, no.

A sigh preceded Darren's next words. "Hello, folks. We live in an age of technology. What we need to do is ditch this truck or find the GPS tracker they obviously put on it."

Jaxon laughed. "You know what, dude. You might be right. Actually I hope you are."

Because, Trent thought grimly, as Thea snuggled deeper into him, if there was no GPS device transmitting their position, then that meant he needed to believe in the impossible. That one of them might inadvertently be a spy.

* * * *

Thea didn't say much from her spot under Trent's arm. What could she add to the conversation other than, despite what Trent and his friends thought, she knew it wasn't a radio type signal giving them away. *It's me.* It had to be.

She knew the things Roderick could do. The fact that she didn't recall him jerking her around to do his will didn't mean he'd not left a nasty surprise in her mind. Or in the mind of others.

While strong in presence and mind, Trent could carry a grain of the parasite's touch, as could his friends. Was she doing the right thing staying with them? If she wasn't the lure drawing the rogues, then was she perhaps safer on her own?

But what if I'm wrong? What if she was the lodestone? Without the guys to protect her against something like Roderick sent tonight, a dark wave of wolves, she wouldn't have lasted thirty seconds.

She preferred to not think about it at all. To let her mind go blank and pretend they'd managed to escape, that the rogues finding them had been a fluke. A coincidence that wouldn't reoccur because of the way Darren, then Marc, and finally Jaxon, drove through the night and most of the next day, changing routes, backtracking, hitting dusty side roads.

The plan to ditch the truck never panned out because they simply didn't have the funds or time to get a new vehicle. They did, however, stop long enough for her to stretch her legs and take care of business. During that short break, they searched the truck bumper to bumper, axle to axle, and found nothing, as she expected.

The first leg of the trip she spent squished up against Trent, a haven that almost made her feel safe. Something about his casual strength and demeanor called to her, and she caved to her need for protection. He wasn't the only one to offer her comfort; when Marc and Darren took a turn in the back, she felt Marc's hands on her ankle and lower legs where she had them tucked up on the seat. But the chest she chose to snuggle against was Darren's. Like Trent, he made her feel safe—among other things.

The ease with which they managed to gain her trust should have made her suspicious. But she ignored the tiny voice warning her in favor of the louder voice that kept repeating, *Ours*. For some reason that sounded right, even if she didn't know what it meant.

Twelve hours of driving later—which meant a sore body sore and eyes gritty from fatigue—they finally stopped to rest. In case their truck did hold a hidden transmitter that they just couldn't find, they parked the truck at a local hardware store then hiked to a motel a few miles away. Well, they walked while Darren carried her, after a token protest on her part.

Hiding in the shadows, they waited while Jaxon booked a room, actually a pair so they could take turns showering and sleeping.

Shown to a room with a pair of beds covered in floral print, she didn't argue too hard when they gave her first dibs on the shower. A new pair of track pants and a T-shirt were a welcome relief, even if they were so huge she could have fit two of herself in them. Wolfing down a dinner comprising a salad, pasta, and garlic bread, she could barely taste the food so quickly did she ingest it. Tummy full, she managed to keep her eyes open only long enough to chew a cookie for dessert.

Tucked in by Darren, and her forehead kissed as he murmured good night, she quickly fell asleep. And dropped into a nightmare.

* * * *

Trent didn't say much when they congregated in the adjoining room, the door separating the spaces open a crack to allow them to hear if anything untoward occurred. As an added precaution, Trent watched through the window, satisfied that the bathroom windows weren't large enough to admit anyone, which meant any attack would come from the front. Despite the fatigue pulling at all of them, they decided to talk. They kept their voices low so as to not wake Thea as they discussed ideas and hashed out plans.

Participating seemed moot to him. He already had his course plotted. Get the biggest fucking gun he could find, return to the mountain, and shoot everything that moved. Twice. Then he'd torch the fucking camp. If there was a vampire hiding under one of the cabins, he'd burn to a crisp, which was kinder than the bastard deserved for messing with his brother.

The time they'd spent in the truck, long hours spent covering their trail, he'd had plenty of time to think. It pissed Trent off to know he'd arrived too late and that David had offed himself when Trent hadn't rescued him in time. *Why couldn't he have held on a little longer?* Anger mixed with chagrin also simmered inside him that he didn't feel more grief at his sibling's passing. He and his brother hadn't been really close growing up; David was a quiet and weak Lycan compared with Trent, who oozed alpha tendencies even from birth. Even though only a few years separated them, Trent veered more into a leader and protector role when it came to interacting with his younger brother, a role his brother resented. When Trent took over the pack upon his father's death, uncontested among their small group, the only one who had a problem with it was the weakest one in the place. Without much explanation other than a feeble, "There's better prospects elsewhere," David had left, and other than a monthly phone call Trent made more out of obligation, he'd not seen much of his brother since. And, until now, not really cared.

Some would have questioned his decision to accept a rogue status to go after his sibling rather than stay safe within the pack. Sure, he and his brother weren't the closest of family or friends, but they shared the same blood. The same mother and father. *I promised Dad I'd take care of him.* No matter his feelings for his younger sibling, Trent owed it to him to look. To rescue if needed. But he'd failed in his quest, and his brother died.

So he was left with only one true option at this point: revenge. The injury done to his brother couldn't go unanswered. He didn't care if Nathan feared the boogeyman he claimed was both his father and a vampire. He didn't give a fuck if Jaxon said the guy was virtually invincible. All things died eventually; some were just tougher than others. *And as my friends know, I am one tough son of a bitch, and I'll be damned if I let Roderick or any other bastard fuck with me or my family.*

A family that now included Thea and her unborn child. His brother's widow. *A woman that draws me against all logic.* Despite his wishes on the matter, he couldn't ignore one basic fact. His wolf clamored to sniff her. Lick her. Claim her. The more it scented her, the more it wanted her. Handling his furry side was easy: Trent held the reins of control. However, he couldn't control his own desire. Much as it appalled him, Trent wanted Thea, too. Wanted to hold her when she cringed so pitifully in the tub. Wanted to kiss the smile that tilted her lips. Enjoyed holding her when she needed comfort, which, in turn, made him want to strip her naked and make her cheeks blush with pleasure instead of embarrassment. He longed to touch her skin, skin his brother had already touched. To go where his brother had already gone.

I don't want to be second! And that was what it boiled down to. No matter his attraction to Thea, no matter how much his beast clamored she belonged to them, the simple truth remained. She'd belonged to David first. She carried *his* child. Trent's nephew. Anything he had with her would always be second. Or third, maybe even fourth if Marc and Darren charmed their way into her heart first. Only a blind man would have missed the scorching glances they bestowed upon her or the way they kept touching her, leaving their scent on her, whether she knew it or not. But their interest didn't bother him too much.

Truthfully, he'd always suspected when he settled down one day that his best friends would probably end up at his side. The best matings were the ones where the males got along. So, honestly, he couldn't argue that hooking up in a foursome with his two best buds and a woman was a bad idea. *But I hate leftovers.*

If he were to allow himself even more truthfulness, he also feared comparison. Would she find him rough compared to David? Less handsome with his more rugged exterior? Less polished because he wasn't as well read? Given a choice, if David had lived, would she have preferred him more? And even more annoying, would she even want Trent at all?

Doubt truly sucked. It made a man want to do rash things. Bold things like staking a claim as her guard. "You can stop arguing about who gets to sleep in the same room as her," he snapped, finally joining the conversation that currently revolved around who would stay in the room with her.

Eyes narrowed and jaws clenched, both Darren and Marc faced him.

"We can't leave her alone," Darren protested.

"Of course not, but given your evident interest in her, you'll never come to an agreement."

"So what do you propose?" Marc asked. "We take turns? Both sleep in the room?"

"Neither. I am going to guard her."

"Why you?" Darren asked as he gave him the evil eye.

"Yeah," Marc added. "Why you?"

"Because she's pregnant with my brother's kid, which makes her family. As head of the family, it's my responsibility to ensure her safety." Oh, yeah, he said that with a straight face, even though it was a huge crock of shit. He just wanted to be close to her, fucked-up feelings, off-limit widow be damned.

"He's got a point," Jaxon interjected with a laugh. "I'm sure he sees her as just a sister."

Trent didn't miss the smirk Jaxon sent his way. "I won't lay a hand on her, if that's what you're both worried about."

"Oh, please," Darren said, stretching the word. "I've seen the way you look at her."

"And it's not like we could miss how you cuddled for most of the trip here."

"I don't cuddle." Why he felt a need to lie when they'd all seen him he couldn't figure out.

"Then what do you call hugging her for hours on end?"

"Offering support to a family member who is frightened. Are we done debating useless shit? 'Cause I, for one, could use some sleep."

"We need to get an early start if we're going to make it to the pack by the weekend."

Whether or not the pack cooperated with the plan they'd concocted remained to be seen.

With not much further ado, Trent slipped into the other room, the soft sound of Thea's breathing easing his wolf as he slid under the covers of the second bed. With her sweet scent enveloping him, he fell into a restless sleep.

Chapter Eight

Head throbbing, Thea woke to find herself in the backseat of David's car. Lifting a hand to her face, she ran fingers over her fat lip and gasped when they came away bloody. Memories of what had happened back at the apartment with David—only it wasn't him—made her scramble to sit upright.

"Rise and shine," he sang from the front, his eyes, still pinpricked with red, peering at her through the rearview mirror. "We're almost there."

"Almost where? Where are you taking me? What the hell do you want?" she cried. She pounded at his shoulders, oblivious to the fact that he drove. He didn't flinch, but he did laugh, a chilling sound that halted her more effectively than violence. She leaned back in the seat and whispered, "What are you?"

"Crazy?" He said it on a questioning note as he swerved the car back and forth across the road. Thea squeaked as she ricocheted side to side.

"Stop it!" she cried. "You'll kill us both."

He didn't reply, instead whistling an off-pitch melody as he careened through the darkness. No lights lit the road they were on, and trees flanked them on both sides, dark sentinels that blurred as he raced along. When he did finally brake, she caught herself just in time on the passenger seat in front of her, the momentum propelling her forward. Before she could count her stars she'd not hit the windshield, David was dragging her out of the back by the hair.

"Let go of me, you psycho," she yelled.

"No. No and no," he sang. "You're coming with me." He continued to tug her painfully across the graveled parking lot to the shadowed treeline.

Pissed at his treatment, and very frightened, she fought him, hitting and scratching, stomping and kicking. None of it freed her, and a headbutt was all it took to knock her out.

When next she woke, she found herself crumpled on a dusty wooden floor. From her prone position, she could see the frayed bottom edge of a plaid couch and a whole family of dust bunnies. *Someone needs to invest in a broom.* An insane thought to match an unreal evening.

Despite the throbbing pain in her head, she pushed herself to her hands and knees then stood. Dizziness made her wobble, and she spent a moment blinking until the room stopped moving. She surveyed the area. No one sat on the sofa or at the scarred Formica table from the seventies behind it. Beyond those relics was an open kitchen, its butcher-block countertop piled high with refuse and dirty dishes, pizza boxes, cans of pop, wrappers, and a plate with something green and fuzzy growing from it.

Not seeing anyone, or an exit—which she really wanted before she ran into crazy David again—she whirled. And screamed!

Standing behind her, silent and unmoving, was a man, a gaunt creature whose skin stretched over the bones of his face, with tufted dark hair sprinkled with silver. But it was his eyes, red and burning, yet his gaze oh so cold, that saw her stumbling back. Fear coursed through every inch of her frame, and she didn't need the churning ball of trepidation in her stomach to know he meant her harm. More frightening, why did she get the impression they'd met before?

The bloodless lips split into a mirthless grin. "Welcome, Thea. I've been expecting you."

"Who are you? How do you know my name? Where's David?"

"I am Roderick, and I know lots of things about you. As for the puppy, I've let him off his leash that he might properly castigate himself for hand-delivering you to me. It's really quite pathetic."

"What are you talking about? Actually, I don't care. I'm leaving."

Brave words that belied the knot in her tummy, a knot that grew in size as she marched with a purpose around the frightening man.

"I don't think so." So softly said, yet the words sent a shiver up her spine.

Spotting a door, she sprinted to it, only to recoil, as he suddenly stood before it. How the hell did he move so fast?

Roderick smiled again. "Leaving so soon? And here we've only just begun to know each other. What do you say we rectify that?"

Before she could answer, he was on her. His fist caught her hair and twisted it. Oh, the pain. She flailed, trying to escape his grasp. He laughed. Motion at the corner of her eye made her pivot. David stood there watching, expressionless.

"Help me!" she cried. "For the love of God, David, help me."

But her lover did nothing but watch. Watched as the monster bit her wrist, the pain of her flesh nothing compared to the agony the monster inflicted on her mind. As David stared on in blatant apathy, she screamed and screamed and screamed, but no one came. And the pain went on forever.

* * * *

The pitiful sounds woke him, choked sobs and thrashing of blankets and limbs from the bed next to his. Trent rose and stared upon Thea. Tears wetted her cheeks. Her lips quivered, and even though she slept, he could smell the fear, the terror.

"What's wrong?" Darren whispered from the

gap in the adjoining door. "I hear crying."

"She's having a nightmare," Trent replied. "Go back to bed. I've got this."

"Are you sure?"

"No. I'm going to let her suffer for no reason. Of course I'm fucking sure."

"Well, excuse me for asking. Shout if you need a hand." Darren eased the door back to its previous position of open just a sliver.

Trent crouched beside the whimpering woman, his conversation with Darren not enough to break her sleep pattern. "Thea, wake up." He spoke low and to no avail. She sobbed. He tried again, a little louder. "Thea. You're having a nightmare. Wake up." Reaching out a hand, he shook her shoulder. And still she cried.

It tore at him. Her obvious misery made him feel helpless. They'd promised her safety, and yet here she suffered. Never mind he couldn't prevent her subconscious from making her relive some of her trauma. He'd failed to protect someone in his care again. But how to wake her? Somehow, shouting and shaking the hell out of her seemed wrong. He didn't want to frighten her more. So what option did that leave?

Sighing, he eased onto the mattress beside her and gathered her into his arms. It felt so damned right, her in his arms, where she belonged. His body noticed, too, and his cock swelled, completely inappropriate considering his intention to ease her, but he couldn't help it. Just like he couldn't help wishing he held her for an entirely different reason. He squashed the naughty urges. She needed him to help her, not get all horned up holding her.

Hugging her against him, he pressed his lips to her temple and made soothing noises. "Hush, beautiful. You're safe now. It's just a nightmare. You need to wake up." It took him several repeats of that mantra before her shudders eased and her cries disappeared. But even when he felt her damp lashes flutter against the curve of his neck, he didn't let go. Didn't want to.

"I-I'm sorry." She hiccupped.

"For what?"

"For waking you up. I was hoping with my escape the nightmares would stop. Guess I was wrong." She sounded so let down.

"You went through a trauma. It's perfectly normal."

"I hate it." She sounded so vehement that a light smile crossed his lips, and he couldn't help pressing it against her forehead. A sigh left her, and more of her tension eased.

"Would it help to talk about it?" *Um, hello?* Had that seriously just left his mouth? In his world, when someone cried, he told them to suck it up. What next? He'd ask her if she wanted to discuss doily making? "Or not. Doesn't matter. But I'll listen if it will help." Dammit. There he went again.

She stopped breathing for a minute before

letting out a big sigh. "You won't like it."

And with that simple phrase, he knew David had played a part in her nightmare. What had his brother done to her? "I'll live. Tell me."

So she did, and as he held her in his arms, he closed his eyes and thanked a god he didn't believe in that David was already dead because, otherwise, he would have had to kill him. Weak-willed or not, there was no excuse for his sibling's action. Her story, sad and infuriating, though, did explain why David had ended up taking his life. After the shame he'd brought upon himself, it was the only solution. Her tale also erased any doubts remaining about the vampire, Roderick. Only an idiot would keep ignoring the evidence.

At the end of her unburdening, he tightened his hug, and she burrowed her face into the hollow under his chin. The way she fit in his arms, against his body, felt so damned right, and alone in bed, his friends in the other room, his body reacted. His cock, dormant during her telling, swelled behind his briefs, bulging against the loose fabric of his track pants. He made sure to keep that area away from her, lest she notice. But, *damn it all*, how he wanted to roll her onto her back and press himself against her.

"Why do I feel so comfortable with you?" she murmured, unaware of his inappropriate lusty thoughts. "When I first met you, all I could think was how you reminded me of David and how scared I was you'd turn out the same way."

"Never. I shouldn't speak bad of the dead, but David was always weak."

She craned her head back until she could see his eyes, her features dimly illuminated by the light she'd left on in the bathroom earlier. "You're not. Even though we've only known each other a day, I bet you'd never let anyone make you do something you didn't want. You're nothing like him."

"Is that a bad thing?" And why did her answer make him taut with suspense.

Her lips curved into a smile. "No. It's good. I like that you're strong. I think it's nice that my baby will have an uncle he can look up to."

And that quickly, the hard-on he'd struggled to keep hidden shriveled. "I should go back to my bed now." He went to move, but she wound her arms around him.

"Please don't go. I know you must think me weak and stupid, but I feel safe with you."

The words froze him. On the one hand, his pride puffed up that she trusted him, but on the other . . . "Why would I think you're weak and stupid?"

"Well, I hooked up so quick with your brother, and even when he changed, I wasn't strong enough to kick him out. Then look what happened. Knocked up. Single and chased by a vampire. I wouldn't say I've exactly made the right choices. I totally fucked up my life."

"No, you haven't. Consider it a rough patch." At her quirked brow, he smiled. "Really rough. But it will pass. We'll kill Roderick and his minions, and then you can start over."

"Yay. That sounds like so much fun," she replied, bitterness in her tone. "I'll have to go on welfare because no one is going to hire a pregnant woman. Then after the baby comes, either I work like a dog so I can pay for rent and daycare or I can stay at home with the child and let the government take care of me. Sounds like a great life."

"No, it—"

"It's okay. You don't have to say anything. I know that was a bitchy thing to say. I should be grateful you and your friends saved me. And I'm sure I'll be fine. It's just so overwhelming right now."

"It doesn't have to be. Things will work out."

"You can't promise that," she replied with a sad smile.

"Actually, I can. This is what's going to happen. You will come back with me when this is all done. You'll live in my house, and I'll take care of you." Once again, he spoke and had no idea who the fuck the sensitive guy was who was putting words in his mouth. Worse, they felt right, and it shocked him to realize he meant them.

"I wasn't asking for your pity."

"I wasn't giving you any. You're carrying all

that's left of my family." He couldn't resist sliding his hand between their bodies to palm her rounded tummy. "I'll care for you both because I want to." *Need to. Protect the pup and the female,* his wolf answered in total agreement.

"I doubt your wife or girlfriend will like that."

"I'm single."

"For now. But what about later? Kind of hard to date with a woman and kid under your roof cramping your style."

"Maybe I've already found what I want." His earlier pep talk to himself about leftovers fled, along with all other logical excuses as to why Thea was wrong for him. *I've known her only a few days.* But it felt as if he'd been waiting for her to arrive forever. *She belonged to David.* And he'd betrayed her, didn't deserve her. *It's too soon.* It couldn't happen soon enough.

Every argument his mind came up with his mind also shot down. Unable to resist, he kissed her, and all he could think was, *she tastes so damned right.*

* * * *

A sane woman would have pushed him away. Slapped him. Kicked him in the nuts. But Thea had lost her sanity a while ago, during her captivity. All she knew was when she woke cradled in Trent's arms, she felt safe. Unafraid. Even as she recounted her experience, she didn't tremble or cry, his soothing presence making it easy for her to unburden herself. He listened, and though David was his brother, he didn't excuse his behavior. He condemned it. Trent took her side, and despite everything that had happened to her, it went a long way to easing her inner pain. Knowing she wasn't alone, that he intended to stand by her and the baby, suddenly made facing the future much easier to bear.

What she found harder to understand was her physical reaction to his presence. Holy heat. Although only their upper bodies touched, and the brush of his lips on her temple left a lingering tingle, arousal blossomed. It baffled and embarrassed her.

Sure, she'd not suffered rape during her incarceration, only the vile gropes when Roderick had first threatened her and the occasional grab since, but still, didn't trauma kill desire? Shouldn't she be in a man-hating mode? Unwilling to trust or get intimate? And she was pregnant with David's kid, and David was Trent's brother. Wasn't it sick to want him? Could pregnant women get horny?

It didn't matter what she thought about it or the reasons crowding her mind against it. According to her hormones, she wanted him—wanted him badly.

So when he kissed her, she didn't do any of the things a normal victim would do. Forget crying, screaming for help, or kneeing him in the balls. Her reaction? She kissed him back. Opened her mouth and invited him in, eager to taste, hungry for more of the fire he ignited with his simple presence. She demanded more, needed more with a frantic urgency because, clasped in his arms, his body fully pressed against hers in all its hard glory, she felt *alive*. Alive in a way she never thought she'd feel again.

It made her aggressive, and she boldly sucked his tongue, quivering when he groaned in reply. Her fingers, caught between their bodies, clutched at his T-shirt, fisting it. Her lower body arched into him, her sex pulsing with wet heat, begging him silently to touch her. He caught the message but didn't give her what she wanted.

He pulled away from her. "We shouldn't do this. You're not thinking clearly."

"This is probably the most clearheaded I've been in weeks," she retorted. "Will you deny me pleasure? Kind of mean seeing as how you started it. And besides, didn't you promise to take care of me?" She tugged his hand down and slid it between their bodies, pressing it against her mound. "I know I'm being brazen, which really isn't like me, but I think I need this, Trent. I need to remember what it feels like to be happy. That not everything is darkness and pain." She kissed him, and he allowed it for a moment before turning his head with a muffled curse.

"Dammit. This is so wrong. I should leave."

Some of her warm buzz faded, and coldness

seeped back in. "I thought you wanted me?" God, she hated how pitiful that sounded.

"I do. Fuck me, but I do. But—"

"It's fine. I understand. I'm a pregnant cow and a slut. I wouldn't want me either." She shut up, lest he hear the tears clogging her throat.

"I never said that."

She pushed at his chest, trying to move away before he spotted the tears brimming in her eyes. *I am such a fucking idiot. What was I thinking?* Why on earth would he want her? Why would anyone? Pregnant and the fucked-up victim of a vampire. What possessed her to think she could have a man like Trent? A man with enough looks and confidence to get any woman he wanted?

"Don't cry," he murmured, his knuckle brushing the moisture clinging to her lashes.

"I'm not," she lied.

Trapped still in the circle of his arms, she couldn't move away when he leaned forward to kiss her lips softly. "You're beautiful, Thea."

"You're just saying that 'cause I'm crying. It's what nice guys do." She sniffled.

"I'm not a nice guy." He flashed her a wicked grin, and a tremulous smile curled her lips.

"Yes, you are. I'm sorry I put you on the spot like that. It won't happen again."

"What if I want it, too? I want you, Thea. I know I should wait and give you some space to heal. I know it's too soon since your ordeal, but, dammit, I still want you."

"Then why push me away?"

"Because we're strangers. Because I'm afraid you'll resent me in the morning for taking advantage. Because . . ." He stopped talking, and a shadow crossed his face.

"Because I slept with your brother first."

He inclined his head.

"I guess that is kind of gross. I'm sorry."

"It's not gross. In my culture, brothers often share a mate, but . . ." He clamped his lips tightly, and she thought he'd stop talking, but instead, he blurted it out in a rush. "David and I are so different. I'm big and rough. I'm not a guy for flowery speeches or shit like that. I don't want to be compared to him."

She heard what he didn't say: *and come up lacking*. "David was a nice guy, at first. I won't lie. But honestly, when he touched me, it didn't feel like my whole body was going to burn to a crisp. You make me want to come and with just a kiss. I don't think you have anything to fear."

"Except for in the morning when you realize you jumped into the sack with a stranger and can't look me in the eye."

She smiled. "And that matters to you?"

"Yeah."

"Most guys would be happy to have a girl pretend it never happened and not try and force a relationship he didn't ask for."

"I'm not most guys, Thea. I'm a wolf. It's different with us."

"Different how? I never did learn much about the whole furry thing other than it's scary to watch."

"There's more to us than our ability to go canine. Most of us live in packs, led by an alpha, the strongest not only physically but mentally overall. We follow a strict set of laws, laws that protect us from discovery and from allowing our base instincts to take over. But some things can't be controlled by rules."

"Like?"

"Mating. Some of our kind get together because of friendship or because our parents arranged it, but some of us, the lucky ones, will meet a woman and instantly know she's meant to be ours."

"How?" she whispered.

"Scent. Instinct. The wolf. We meet the right woman, and we want her. Need her."

"For sex?"

"Sex that lasts a lifetime. When a wolf meets his female, he claims her. Marks her with a bite, and she in turn bites him back, completing a blood circle that binds them forever."

"Why are you telling me this?" A chill went through her as she touched the scar on her neck, a faint impression of teeth that had never faded after David bit her their first time.

"My brother mated you," he answered before she could question.

"How could he? I never said *yes*."

"Wolves don't often ask. We just do."

"But I never bit him back, so how could we be mated?"

"You didn't?"

She shook her head.

"Didn't you have an urge to?"

Held by his brother, the conversation infinitely weird, she should have shied from it but didn't because she was finally getting answers, whether she liked them or not. "No. I was attracted to him. There was a little spark, but that's about it. He bit me. I kind of freaked, and he apologized. End of story. So what does it mean?"

"I'm not sure. I've never heard of a half-mating before. Speaking of sparks, what do you feel when I touch you?"

A blush heated her cheeks. "I don't know if we should keep talking about this."

"You feel it, don't you? Almost like an electrical current?"

She nodded.

"I feel the same thing. I have since the moment we first touched. I saw you, and despite everything going on, I want to pick you up and run away with you. Protect you."

"Because of the baby."

"No. Because of you. You're my mate, Thea. I know it might be hard for you to handle, especially with everything else, but knowing you're my mate is why I can't make love to your body. Why I can't pleasure you. Why I sound like such a fucking dork."

"I don't think you sound dorky." She smiled.

"Yeah, I do. Trust me, I usually have the mouth of a trucker, even around women. I don't say nice, thoughtful things. Or talk about feelings and shit."

"Why?"

"Because I hadn't met the right woman before, I guess. I hadn't met you, which is why you need to take the time to think this through. Because of who we are, we can't just fuck—no matter what our bodies say."

"I don't understand." He wanted her, but didn't because of some weird culture thing?

"Once we have sex, there will be no going back. No morning-after regret. I will claim you. You will be mine, which means forever."

"And you're not sure?"

"Oh, I am. I don't need to date you for a week, a month, or a year to know you're the one I've waited for. But you don't have that certainty yet. You want to feel alive. Have me touch you and fuck you, but when the morning comes, are you prepared for the fact I won't be able to let you walk away?"

"This is insane."

"Which is why I stopped."

"No, not your story. Just, I wondered why I felt this way. I knew it wasn't normal for me to want a guy so badly. To ignore everything that's happened to me. And now you're telling me there's a reason for it. It's kind of reassuring, actually."

"You feel it, too?"

"I think so, only . . ." She chewed her lip.

"Only what?"

She dropped her voice to the barest whisper. "This is going to sound horrible, but maybe I'm wrong because I feel it for Darren, too. And, to a much lesser extent, Marc."

She waited for his anger and his disgust. Instead, he laughed. "I'm sure that will make them happy when they hear."

"Okay, I think I missed something."

"Oh, shit, how to explain this without making it sound like we're perverts."

"Now I'm really worried."

"There are more males than female Lycans. Because of the vast difference in this ratio, the council adopted a policy hundreds of years ago that states females must take a minimum of two mates up to a maximum of four."

"That's barbaric!"

"Yes, which is why the current council is trying to change the laws. They're managed to a certain extent. Now the women get a choice in who their mates will be instead of having their parents or their alpha choose for them."

"The men are okay with sharing?"

"We're raised with the knowledge so most of us deal with it well enough."

"And because I get that electroshock thing and stuff with Darren, you think he's supposed to be my fated mate, too, or something?"

"Yes. And possibly Marc, too."

The concept stunned her—aroused her. "It doesn't bother you?"

"I'll admit a part of me is jealous. No man finds it easy to share his female, but then again, the pleasure that can be found in a group . . ." He smiled suggestively, and she blushed.

"At the same time?" she squeaked. "Oh, I don't think so."

"It's not necessary. Many groupings choose to keep things one-on-one, but there are others who prefer to tread that racier edge."

She buried her face against his chest, her heart racing, as she couldn't help picturing what it would be like to have another man in bed with her and Trent. More than one set of hands touching. Numerous mouths sucking. The decadence of it brought her arousal flaring back, and she found herself rubbing her cheek against his chest, cursing the fabric that separated them.

"What are you doing? Didn't you hear what I said?"

"I did," she murmured as she tugged at his shirt, pulling it up so she could touch him. She darted out her tongue and licked his smooth flesh.

"Thea," he growled.

"I thought I was going to die. I never thought

I'd see sunshine or another sane person again. I never thought I'd *feel* again. For all I know, Roderick could find us and kill us all."

"He won't!"

"Anything could happen, and I am not going to take a chance on missing out. So what if I don't get this whole werewolf and mated thing? So what if it's forever? I'll take the chance you snore and leave your socks on the floor. Life is too precious to waste it wondering if it's the right thing." She kissed her way up to his jaw, and he sighed.

"Are you sure? This shouldn't be taken—"

She swallowed the rest of his words. Logic had no place here, not right now, probably not ever. Things had changed. The world she knew no longer existed, and she meant what she said. She could die tomorrow. Or he could. Right now, this moment, was theirs, if they chose to take it. And, dammit, she burned for his touch.

Thankfully, he chose not to fight any longer and, with a groan of surrender, kissed her back. Even better, he rolled her onto her back, his heavy body atop hers, his groin nestled between her legs, pressing against her. She gasped into his mouth as he ground himself against her, rubbing against the source of her arousal. She clutched his shoulders with digging fingers, arching her hips into his thrusts, the fabric separating them acting as a sensual enhancer.

The kiss ended so he could trail fiery kisses

down her neck, nipping at her skin, drawing forth tiny cries. His hot mouth captured the peak of a breast through her shirt, sucking at her nipple, the pleasure of it sending jolts to her sex, which clenched in reply. His hand slid between their bodies, making its way under the waistband and dragging through her curls. He touched her, and he caught her cry with his mouth. Kissed her passionately while his finger rubbed against her clit, spiraling her pleasure higher and higher.

"Yes!" she keened. She screamed into his mouth as she came, tremors of her pleasure shaking her body. And still she wanted him. Wanted him inside her. With frantic hands, she pushed at his pants, but he caught them and forced her to look him in the eyes.

"Are you sure? Last chance to say *no*."

And he thought he wasn't a nice guy. It seemed he didn't know himself. "I need you. Please."

He answered her with another torrid kiss, his hands helping her to yank down his pants. His cock sprang from its confinement, hot and hard. She clasped it and stroked. Chuckled wantonly at his hiss of pleasure.

"If you keep doing that, I won't make it inside you."

"We can't have that." She released him, and his body nestled between her legs, the head of his shaft unerringly finding the entrance to her sex. He teased her, though, inching only a piece in, enough to make her mewl and squirm.

It was his turn to chuckle, a masculine sound that sent shivers through her heated body. "What's wrong, beautiful? Need something?"

"You're a tease."

He retreated and rubbed the head of his cock against her clit. "Yeah. What are you going to do about it?"

She nipped his chin. He growled. She moved to his neck, licking and nibbling until he thrust into her. Oh, sweet heavens. Her teeth clamped down harder on the skin of his neck as he pistoned her, and as she continued to bite, a little voice in her head urging her to press down harder, his own mouth opened over the skin of her shoulder. He caught her in an identical grip, the sharp pain of his bite making all her muscles tighten, and when he clamped down harder, she squeezed her teeth tightly as she came.

The orgasm hit her harder than the first, slamming into her body and leaving her shuddering as his body continued to pump into hers. She had only a moment to realize she'd drawn blood, the metallic taste on her tongue, when he came and another climax rocked her, leaving her mouth open wide on his skin in a silent scream that, if audible, would have surely shattered glass. More of his blood seeped into her mouth, and she inadvertently swallowed.

A jolt went through her, a moment of hyper-awareness where she felt emotions, not only hers but . . . his. His deep satisfaction. His need for her. His fear, also for her. For a moment in time, they shared one mind, one body, one soul. It was glorious.

Muscles limp, body sated, and, for some reason, ridiculously happy—*probably because I came three times*—she snuggled into him when he rolled to his side, still holding her. Cocooned in his arms and with the edges of his emotions tickling hers, she fell asleep, and the nightmare stayed away.

* * * *

Marc listened through the crack in the door. He couldn't help himself. A part of him was jealous and, yes, a little mad that Trent was moving in on Thea so quickly, especially after his bullshit of "I need to watch her 'cause I'm family.'" But honestly, if anyone had a right to first claim on David's widow, then it was Trent. The guy would never say it aloud, but despite not having a hand in it, he'd blame himself for what happened. Marc expected he would have fought his attraction to Thea longer, though, but then again, who could have resisted her soft and aroused *please*? Hell, Marc had almost gone in there on his knees to beg a turn.

Probably not a good idea given they didn't know yet how she felt about having a mate, let alone more than one, although Trent had bitten the bullet and come clean with her, telling her how it worked in the pack. Even better, she hadn't freaked and said no way. They should be so lucky. But after that part of the conversation, it proved hard to remain a silent watcher, and he moved away, trying to distract himself, only to find himself back at the door again minutes later. And they were done talking.

That lucky bastard Trent was doing something that drew the most delicious cries from her. Marc peeked through the open crack, not seeing much other than Thea's legs wrapped around Trent's flanks, eagerly inviting him into her body. Fuck, how he wanted to join in, catch her cries with his lips, stroke her nub as Trent fucked her, making her even more wild. He abstained, knowing it was too soon. But it didn't stop him from getting horny. He would have stroked himself if he wasn't so aware of Jaxon sharing the room behind him. Forget Darren. They'd tag-teamed girls before, and while they didn't touch each other, pretty much everything else was fly.

"Did he mark her?" The whispered query came from Darren, who'd risen from the bed to stand watch at the window.

Marc turned to face him. He nodded.

"Damn. That was quick and probably for the best. This will create a bond between them that will help them both heal from David's betrayal."

How mature of Darren to note that. It did

nothing for Marc's raging erection, though.

"Think he'll want to share?" Marc asked in a low voice as he joined his pack brother at his post.

"Law says he has to if she agrees."

"True. Think she will?"

Darren shrugged.

"I hope so." Doubt. A new emotion for Marc and one he didn't quite know how to banish. "And if she's not sure, we'll have to show her the benefits."

"Naked, I assume?"

Marc chuckled. "Is there any other way?"

"Have I mentioned I like how your mind works?"

"Have I mentioned a need for sleep?" Jaxon growled, interrupting them. "Plan your gangbang when we're awake and I'm not around. Some of us don't exactly have the privilege of being with our mate."

"Sorry." Marc wondered how Jaxon survived the separation. He'd heard of some mated pairs going a little crazy when they were apart too long. It was also why matings with more than one male were encouraged because it meant one could always keep the female company if the other had to leave for any length of time for work or other matters. Depression was something they had to watch for otherwise. He wondered if the fact that Jaxon had only exchanged bites with Bailey and not sex allowed him to cope. *That or he's got a wicked grip on his hand by now.*

Poor guy. Of them all, he probably wanted vengeance against the vampire the most. He'd lost everything. Pack. Friends. His mate. At least Marc had his brothers of the fur and a woman he'd do his best to claim. *I don't know if I could survive alone.* Hopefully, he'd never find out.

Chapter Nine

As she woke the next morning, Thea waited for the shame to hit her. *I slept with a guy I barely know.* A guy she already felt closer to than the man who'd fathered her child. A man who gave her honesty and a choice. A wolf who had marked her and, according to his words, made her his mate. *His forever.*

A sane person would have wondered if she'd dreamed it all, imagined the strange conversation and climatic sex. Who could refute it, though, with the evidence blatant in the way she was splayed across half of his naked chest, her head nestled on him, using him like a pillow, his arms wrapped snugly around her? It stirred her desire to life, which surprised her. Mornings weren't her forte.

Listening to his heart, which beat steadily, she again focused on her feelings. Did she feel shame at what she'd done? Oddly, no. Would he? Totally different question. According to his speech in the middle of the night, they were now irrevocably tied. Would he still feel that way in the light of day? A part of her wanted to wake him up and find out. But first she needed to take care of business. How could she escape to brush her teeth, take care of a full bladder, and run a comb through her hair without waking him and introducing him to her not-so-pretty morning self?

"I know you're awake." His chest rumbled under her cheek as he spoke.

"How?"

"Your breathing pattern changed."

"Oh. Have you been awake long?"

"A while."

"Sorry. I know I have a tendency to crowd the bed. David used to get so mad." She wanted to slap herself as soon as the words left her mouth.

"Well, I happen to like it. It makes it easier to do this." He slid her fully on top, and she gasped as the hard nudge of his cock let her know just how much he did like it.

She pushed herself to a sitting position, letting his cock bob up behind her ass cheeks, and peered down at him. "I shouldn't have said that."

"Said what? The thing about David? Don't worry about it. I told you. The pack does relationships a little differently. So I'm not going to fly into a jealous rage if that's what you're afraid of. And I don't expect you to forget him."

"Even if a part of me wants to?"

A heavy sigh left him. "I can't really blame you for that. But despite his weakness, before David met Roderick, he wasn't a bad guy."

"I know. And in time, I might manage to

forgive and forget what he became. I guess I'll have to for the baby." She rested her hand on her stomach, and he covered it with his, the warm press of his callused palm making her tummy flutter.

He caught her gaze, a smoldering stare that brought a flush to her body that had everything to do with arousal and the remembrance of how he'd touched her the night before.

"I'm glad to see you're not trying to run away or hide," he said. "I kind of wondered if you would."

A chuckle slipped past her lips. "I wondered, too. But it's weird. I feel so totally comfortable with you. Like we've known each other forever."

"It's the mating bond. You might even sense some of my emotions and, in some cases, know where I am."

Before she could ask him more about the whole mating thing, her stomach growled, a loud, insistent noise that made her cheeks heat with embarrassment.

"Sounds like someone is hungry." He grinned, the carefree expression taking the hard edges away from his face. "Why don't you hop in the shower while I go grab us something to eat?"

"No eggs, please. They and my pregnancy don't agree with each other." She shuddered, and he laughed. He rolled her to lie under him and gave her a hard kiss before getting up and strutting naked to the bathroom. She lay on her back, a smile on her lips.

Maybe things will turn out all right.

A shower, pee, and a thorough brushing of her teeth later, she emerged in a towel and squeaked. She clutched the damp fabric to her closely, and Darren, who lounged in a chair, grinned.

"Sorry I startled you. Marc left to get breakfast. Trent needed to pick up some untraceable cell phones, and we didn't want to leave you alone."

"Where's Jaxon?"

"Showering. He fell asleep last night before his turn. And given the way his nerves are shot this morning, I don't expect we'll see him until he's completed his part of the plan."

"Which is?"

"Convincing his mate to take you in just in case Nathan, the pack alpha, refuses."

"Did you guys spend a lot of time planning last night after I flaked?" She asked this idly while wondering how she could grab her pants discreetly and run back to the bathroom to dress before Trent arrived and saw her conversing practically naked with his friend.

"Some. But we can fill you in on that later when we're all together. I hear congratulations are in order?"

"Excuse me?"

Darren stood and strode toward her, and she backed up until her butt hit the wall. He kept coming until he towered over her, a half-smile curling his lips. "You mated with Trent. You're part of our pack now. Welcome." She couldn't move away with him crowding her and, with his hand tilting her chin to turn her face up, couldn't avoid his lips when they brushed over hers. A tingle spread through her, heating her body and curling in her tummy.

This is so wrong. How could she desire another man after what she'd shared with Trent?

She placed her palms against his chest, meaning to push him away, but he pressed closer, his tongue slipping past the barrier of her lips to slide along hers. A languorous sensation spread through her, rendering her limbs wobbly, not that she could fall with his body pinning her in place.

"Breakfast." Trent's announcement acted like a cold bucket of water. She turned her head sideways, breaking off the kiss and shoved at Darren.

"It's okay," he murmured.

"No, it's not," she hissed.

"What's wrong?" Trent asked, coming alongside them.

Darren still hadn't moved, and Thea vacillated between embarrassment and anger.

The moment demanded she speak. "I didn't kiss him."

"Then what do you call the lip-lock I walked in on?" Trent asked wryly.

"My doing," Darren said, fessing up. "I was congratulating her on the mating and welcoming her to the pack." Darren finally moved away and clasped Trent in a hug, patting his back with hard thumps.

Thea inched away, still clutching at her towel. "Do all welcomes include tongue?" she snapped, not sure why Trent's lack of reaction bothered her.

The men separated, and both eyed her. "You enjoyed it," Darren announced.

"Did not."

Trent shook his head. "I can smell you did, beautiful. It's okay. I told you last night, in the pack, females take more than one mate. Darren is just stating his interest in being one. And I wouldn't be surprised if Marc does something soon to stake a claim, too."

"You were serious about that? But we just hooked up. And who says I want three guys? I don't even know if I can handle you, Trent, let alone your buddies."

"You don't need to handle us. We'll *handle* you. Just imagine, three guys means three times the pleasure," Darren replied with a wicked grin.

Now there was a visual to make her cross-eyed and weak-kneed. "This is so wrong," she moaned.

"Only by human morals. In our world, it's totally normal and expected."

"It's okay, Thea," Trent murmured before

dipping his head to brush her lips. "This changes nothing between us."

"How can it not?" she exclaimed.

"Because this is how it works in the pack. And if I have to share you with anybody, I'd rather it be with men that I count as friends. Men whom I know and trust."

"I need to sit down," she mumbled, heading to a chair. She halted before sitting, realizing she still wore the damned towel. With a growl of annoyance, she snagged her pants off the floor and entered the bathroom to change into them and the T-shirt she'd removed before her shower. *God, I hope we can get some real clothes soon.* Underwear and a bra would have been nice for starters.

When she emerged for the second time, all the guys but Jaxon were in the room. Nobody said a word, but as she walked to the chair left for her at the table, she couldn't help feeling like everyone stared at her. Judged her. *Yeah, I slept with Trent.* Something they all seemed to know. But, dammit, she had no plans to sleep with his buddies. Awesome kiss or not. Weird pack rules or not.

Getting involved in a four-way orgy wasn't high on her list of priorities. According to the guys, they were still in danger. She needed to get somewhere safe and take care of herself and the baby. She also needed time to adjust to the fact, according to them, that she was a wolf or at least part wolf.

I don't need distractions in the form of three too-sexy-for-their-own-good men. Although, in the case of Trent, it was too late to go back. Him, she'd keep. But that was it. No matter what they thought.

None of her thoughts were spoken aloud, and she watched them as she chewed. They seemed oblivious to the mental turmoil they'd put her through, laughing and joking amongst themselves. Tossing her the occasional wicked grin or teasing smile. It didn't help her mental mindset.

Why, oh why, do I feel like getting naked and telling them breakfast is on me?

* * * *

Darren could see the conflict on Thea's face. He'd not meant to cause it, but when she emerged from the bathroom looking so tempting and sexy wearing just a towel and damp skin, he couldn't resist. He kissed her on a flimsy pretext, and despite her words of protest, she enjoyed it. He'd not missed how her heart raced and her body softened, accompanied by the sweet smell of her arousal.

Chagrin, though, did claim him a bit when he saw her upset at getting caught by Trent. Actually, a part of him had worried for a moment, too. It was one thing to share regular human girls and to preach pack law; it was another to confront it. Some males who found and claimed their mates experienced difficulties in the beginning when it came to sharing. Lucky for Darren, it looked as if Trent had already come to terms with it. Now they just had to convince Thea. Had to because, despite having only met her a few days ago, Darren wanted to make her his, badly.

"So are we still on board for the plan?" Jaxon asked, finally joining them and grabbing his breakfast of a breakfast sandwich and hash browns. He took a sip of his coffee as he waited for confirmation.

Trent frowned. "What makes you think the pack will go for it? It means putting the spotlight on them where Roderick is concerned."

"Roderick already has his sights on them because of his son, Nathan," Jaxon replied. "Nathan would do anything to end the travesty that wears his father's body."

"But what about the rest of the pack?" Marc chewed on a stirring stick that had come with the coffees. "Just because Nathan might want to do something crazy to kill the vampire doesn't mean the rest of the pack will go along."

Jaxon laughed. "Have you met Nathan? That guy is a true-blue alpha who's only gotten stronger since he discovered the truth about his father. If he says jump off a cliff to his pack, they'll run and do it without question."

"He didn't manage to convince me to stay, even when he threatened me with rogue status," Trent supplied.

A sly smile tilted Jaxon's lips. "As if a temporary member of his pack, who is an alpha in his own right, would so easily bow to the dictates of another. Give me a break. When I said *his pack*, I meant those he led before the curfews and the merging of the groups for safety."

"So who's going to call him?" Darren asked.

Trent sighed. "I am."

"And I'll make my own phone call and see if Bailey and her boys can't do something for Thea," Jaxon said with a grimace.

Darren caught the flash of pain on his face and felt sorry for the guy, but not sorry enough to stop him from his task. Thea needed a haven before the vampire caught up to them. As for Darren and his buds, once they had her squared away, they were going hunting.

Chapter Ten

The house phone rang, the digital display showing a number she didn't recognize. Bailey answered.

"Hello."

Nothing. A silence broken only by static hummed in her ear, but of more interest, the scar in her lip tingled. "Jaxon?" she whispered, her heart stuttering to a halt. "Is that you?" For a moment, only more static greeted her. Then . . .

"Hi, sweet cheeks."

Suddenly boneless, she slumped into a chair. For a moment, pure shock kept her silent. Not for long. "Oh my God. You're alive. I knew it. I knew you didn't die. But where are you? Where have you been? Why haven't you called?" she accused. Left unsaid was, *why didn't you return?* They both knew how impossible that was.

"I've been here and there. Trying to atone for my actions. Not succeeding as well as I'd hoped."

Closing her eyes, she let herself drink in the sound of his voice. He spoke with a weariness that made her ache, ache for the man who used to laugh all the time, the man who sounded so alone. "Are you the one who's been killing rogues before the extermination teams arrive and spoiling everyone's fun?"

A chuckle rumbled through the earpiece, and she smiled at this ghost of his former self even as tears filled her eyes at the wry twist. "Maybe."

"It's dangerous."

"It's necessary," he countered. "I would do anything to help keep you safe."

He'd already proven that when he dove off the cliff with Roderick, saving her and the others. "I miss you, Jaxon. I miss you so much, and I know they won't say it, but the guys miss you, too."

"They miss the fact they haven't been able to kill me yet."

"No! They—"

"You don't need to lie, sweet cheeks. I know they hate me, and with good reason. I betrayed them and you. Because of me, you got hurt. You could have died. I'd hate me, too, if I were in their shoes."

"Isn't there a way to fix this? I want you to come home. To me. Although you might not be too impressed. I'm the size of a house now."

"I bet you look beautiful no matter your size," he softly whispered. "And I miss you, too. I dream of you every night. But that's all we can have now. Dreams. There is no forgiveness for me, only revenge against the one who did this, which is why I'm calling. I know I don't have the right to ask, but I need a favor."

"Anything."

"There's a girl."

"Really?" Bailey couldn't help the jealous lilt of her question.

"Not my girl, so don't start growling, sweet cheeks. She belongs to some friends I made. She was Roderick's prisoner until we rescued her."

"Oh, the poor thing."

"Yeah. She's a little traumatized, but strong. Thing is, we think Roderick did to her what he did to you. Somehow, he's woken her wolf side."

"Has she changed yet?"

"No. And she won't for a while, I'd wager, because she's also pregnant."

The news rocked her. She'd suffered in Roderick's care, the vampire somehow bringing forth a heritage she'd never known existed. The first time she shifted was not an experience she wished on anyone. *The poor girl.* "Who's the father?"

"He's dead. It was his brother and his buddies that rescued her when they came looking."

"Are you talking about Trent, Marc, and Darren? Wyatt and Gavin came back from a meeting with Nathan a while ago talking about how this guy and his friends left to look for his brother. Nathan had to declare them rogue because of it, which seems kind of extreme."

"That's them. And Nathan had to do it. He's the one who advocated the curfew and combining of the packs for strength. To have someone leave in blatant disregard for the decree would have made him look weak."

"He could have sent a squad of fighters with them." Although Bailey respected Nathan as a leader, not an easy position to maintain with the large number of males, testosterone making some of them brash. Still, she didn't always agree with his decisions.

"And they would have gotten in the way of the search. Roderick's smart. He's got spies, obviously, because how many of our raids has he escaped from? Trent's best bet was going as a small group. Distract the rogues, a quick in and out, taking out a few rogues on the way."

"What happened to the brother? You said he was dead."

"Yeah, he didn't fare so well as the object of Roderick's mind games and killed himself before Trent found the vampire's lair. I met up with Trent and his buddies about a day after I located their camp. We were too late to rescue David, but we managed to rescue the girl, and we've escaped for the moment. But—"

She finished his sentence. "Roderick will want her back. We can't let him have her, Jaxon."

"I know, which is why I'm calling. Trent's talking to Nathan right now. We've got a plan, but I want you to do something for me."

"Tell me what you need."

"I need you." The soft admission whispered across the phone line, and her heart stuttered. It felt so good to speak to Jaxon again, but at the same time, it broke her heart. She missed him so much but couldn't see him. Touch him. Tell him face-to-face she forgave him. Still loved him.

It'll never happen. She tried anyway. "Come home, Jaxon."

"I can't." He spoke again in a deeper, emotionless tone that failed because she knew it meant he cared too much. "My real reason for calling is to warn you. We're going to try and get the girl sent to the pack. Trent's talking to Nathan right now. If he agrees, we'll drop her off."

"Nathan won't go for it."

"He might. She'd need to stay under guard for obvious reasons, but if Nathan likes our plan, he'll need her close at hand."

"Hold on a second. By putting her in our midst, won't you be painting a bull's-eye on the pack?" Dangling bait at Roderick?

"If there were any other group big enough or strong enough to take her instead, I'd beg, but our pack with its size and cadre of males is our best chance for this to work. I mean we get not just Nathan and his strength but also all the lesser alphas with him, along with the betas. No other pack has that kind of power. Most can't hold them together."

"Nathan holds them together with that big voice of his and his fist."

"Welcome to the world of a Lycan. No matter how evolved we are, it all comes down to

'I will beat the crap out of you if you don't toe the line.'"

"It's archaic."

"But it works."

"That it does. But enough of how Lycans have thick heads and short fuses, you still haven't told me what you need. There's nothing I can say that will convince Nathan to take her or not."

"I know. And while I promised Trent I'd ask you to intervene, I actually need something entirely different from you."

"Anything."

"You have to get to safety. You need to convince the guys to leave with you and go into hiding."

"Why would I do that? Leave the protection of the pack and the gated compound? Are you nuts?" She didn't say it, but judging by the silence, he understood the unspoken, *Is Roderick giving you orders again?* Immediately, guilt slapped her.

"I'm not crazy or possessed. I hope. My theory is somehow, the blood I inadvertently swallowed made me immune to his mind games. So no worries on that score. But forget about me, I need you to leave because I couldn't stand it if our plan failed and you end up back in his clutches."

"It won't happen. This place is better guarded than that secret place they hide all the gold. And, besides, I know you won't let anything happen to me."

"Don't say that," he growled.

"Say what? That I trust you?"

"You shouldn't."

"Too bad. I do. And I'm not going anywhere."

"Please, sweet cheeks." He begged her, and she bit her lip. She hated to cause him such misery when he already suffered enough.

But to hide like a coward? "No."

"What's it going to take to convince you to go?"

There was one thing he could do. "Meet me."

"What?"

"You heard me. Meet me. I want to see you. Touch you. Look you in the eyes."

"It's too dangerous."

"So is leaving the safety of the pack," she retorted.

"I can't come to you, and they'll never let you leave the compound alone. Wyatt, Gavin, and Parker will forbid it."

"They are not the bosses of me."

"They are of your safety. Where you go, they go, so if we meet, they'll see me and kill me."

Ah, yes, her overprotective mates. Jaxon was right. They would probably cause him grievous harm. They found it hard to forgive Jaxon his actions, but mostly, she thought they didn't forgive themselves for not suspecting—and deeper down wondered if it could have happened to them. "So we meet in a public place, full of humans. Even they wouldn't dare try something then."

A heavy sigh came through the receiver. "You're not going to budge, are you?"

"Nope. You want me to run, then you meet me."

"You drive a hard bargain, sweet cheeks. I'll call you in a few days with a time and place."

The resignation in his tone almost made her reconsider. But she had to see him. "I love you, Jaxon."

"You shouldn't, Bailey. Stay safe." The line went dead, and the dam holding her emotions burst. The tears poured down her cheeks, in relief because now she knew he lived. Tears of joy because she'd get to see him. And finally tears of wretched misery because the possibility of getting him back into her life was a big fat zero.

And that's so unfair. Everyone deserved a second chance.

* * * *

Nathan hung up the phone and leaned back in his office chair. On days like these, the mantle of alpha and leader hung heavy.

"What's wrong?" Dana, his mate and the love of his life, came into the room and draped herself on his lap. Her hands cupped his cheeks and tilted his face until she could see his eyes.

"I just finished talking to Trent."

"The guy who left to find his brother?"

He nodded, unsmiling, for the situation with Trent and his friends still preyed on him. He'd labeled the men rogue, had to lest anyone call him weak. But, dammit, how he'd wanted to do the opposite and help them. Help them strike back against his twisted father. Their current stalemate with Roderick chafed, but experience had taught him that the vampire seemed to know one step in advance what they planned. So even though it burned him to do it, it was safest for Trent and the others to leave as a small group, outcasts to any prying eyes. They'd only partially succeeded.

"And?" Dana, impatient as ever, snapped her fingers to draw him from his musings. "What happened? Did they find anything?"

"Trent's brother is dead, along with a bunch of other rogues under Roderick's dominion. They're heading back in this direction now."

"Let me guess. He wants back into the pack, even though he came in contact with the vampire. You know we can't allow that."

"Of course we can't. It's not what he was asking. Well, not for himself at any rate. They rescued a girl, a human girl, carrying a Lycan babe."

Popping to her feet, Dana paced around him. "Another dormant like Bailey? How did Roderick find her?"

"Does it matter? He did, and she's pregnant, even though her wolf hasn't fully emerged."

After halting, she pivoted on a heel and narrowed her gaze. "So he called just to tell you?"

"No. He wants us to offer sanctuary to the girl."

"Too dangerous," Dana replied quickly. "It was pure luck that Bailey wasn't infected by Roderick, and even now, we still have people watching her and her mates just in case. I know you haven't forgotten what Jaxon did."

Who could? The shock of it still haunted his friends Gavin, Parker, and Wyatt—not to mention their mate still pined for the betrayer. "Speaking of whom, Trent ran into Jaxon while tracking his brother down. They teamed up to invade the rogue camp."

"Are they insane? After what Jaxon did, what would possess them to trust him?"

A shrug lifted his shoulders. "According to Trent, Jaxon seems to be his own man, determined to take Roderick down."

"Or so he says," she replied suspiciously.

A suspicion he shared. "Trent says he questioned Jaxon on that because, at first, he didn't trust a word he said. Jaxon claims when he fought Roderick's control on the cliff, he bit him and tasted some of his blood. According to him, it did a few things. One, he always has a general sense of where Roderick is, and, two, it seems to have made him immune to the mind thing."

"Again, so he says."

"I get it. You don't trust him."

Dana planted a hand on her cocked hip and pursed her lips. "Don't tell me you do? Let's say for a moment Jaxon did manage to free himself from the monster. We still can't take the others back, not knowing they might carry ticking time bombs in their heads."

"They don't want to come back. They just want us to take the girl. They've got a plan to try and deal with Roderick. But they need my help, and they want the girl safe while they implement it."

"Is their plan any good?"

Nathan smiled. "It's better than what we've accomplished so far, which is nothing. It's bold. Carries risk. But—"

"We can't keep living like this. Emerging only in the sunshine and hiding from the shadows. We're wolves. We're meant to run free."

"Exactly. And to be quite honest, their idea's the best I've heard in a while." Especially since their attempts to deal with the vampire and rogue problem didn't seem to get better, no matter how many twisted wolves they killed. As for Roderick, he continually slipped through their grasp. And that Nathan couldn't live with. As the son of the monster, he knew it was only a matter of time before his undead father came looking for him. Came gunning for his family. *I won't allow Dana or my child to be hurt.*

"So what do we need to do?"

A grimace crossed his face because he just knew his feisty mate wouldn't like the next part. "I need to set up a meeting with the vampires and see if they'll help us kill Roderick or at least give us a weakness we can exploit."

Dana resumed her pacing. "No fucking way. You are not meeting with them."

"Someone has to."

"Then it can be someone else, dammit! What if they can control you like Roderick does with the others?"

Nathan shook his head. "I think that's a specialty reserved for my father. Don't you think we'd know by now if vampires could control wolves? We've heard plenty of stories about it happening to humans."

"Old wives' tales and legends that, up until a few years ago, we thought were make-believe."

"But as you well know, most legends have a kernel of truth. I believe the vampires have no use for us because they can't control us. Roderick is an anomaly because he started out as a Lycan."

"Fine. You want to meet with the bloodsuckers. How? How are you going to find them? It's not like we have an address."

"Yeah, this is where it gets tricky. Trent says we should try placing an ad in the paper."

Dana smirked. "Oh, yes. I can see that working. Hey, vampire dudes, alpha wolf wants to meet to discuss how to kill your kind. P.S.: BYOB. Bring your own blood."

A chuckle escaped him, despite the gravity of the conversation. Dana grinned, too, before flopping back on his lap and twining her arms around his neck.

"What would I do without you?" he murmured as he nuzzled her neck.

"Whack off a lot."

He snorted against her skin. "Such a lady."

"Oh, shut it. You love that I know how to get down and dirty."

"That I do," he agreed even as she found his lips for a hot kiss.

He allowed himself to enjoy her distraction for a moment before he pulled away with regret. "I still have to do this."

She made a moue of annoyance. "I was hoping you'd forget."

"You would have needed to start farther south then," he replied with a wink and leering smile.

Laughter shook her. "Note taken. Fine. If I can't convince you it's a bad plan, then let's at least make sure we go about this in a way that doesn't leave us too exposed and keeps you safe."

"Safety will only come when Roderick is vanquished. So, now that you're planning to help, how should we word this ad so that we don't attract the wrong sorts?"

"I thought we were the wrong sort."

"Dana!" He said her name while laughing. She knew how to draw him out of his moods.

She chuckled. "Leave it to me. I'll design something guaranteed to have the vamps running for a phone."

"While you do that, I'm going to call in the guys in charge of defense."

"Aren't you worried about showing your hand to the spy?"

Nathan grinned. "I saw a movie that gave me a great idea. I'm going to start several rumors, all of them about Roderick."

"There's already a half-dozen, so that won't be hard. What about that girl, though? Bringing her in is still risky."

"I know, which is why I'm rejecting that part of their plan." And not just because she posed a danger to his people. The plan called for bait, and while Nathan didn't have a problem sticking his neck out as a tempting morsel to draw his father in, it wouldn't hurt to have backup. Not that he would tell Trent that. A man newly mated wasn't likely to want to risk his female, whether it was for the good of the pack or not. It was up to an alpha to make the hard decisions.

"You'll refuse even though she's pregnant?"

As usual, Dana pinpointed the one thing that gave even Nathan pause. Could he condemn both mother and child for something that wasn't their fault? Sacrifice them for the greater good of his pack?

I'd sacrifice a hell of a lot more to keep my family safe.

"She's pregnant with a rogue's baby while under the influence of a vampire. Who knows what kind of monster she carries. I can't risk it."

"They won't like it."

"Too fucking bad. I rule this pack and the council. They should count themselves lucky I'm willing to even help. And if they don't like it, then they're welcome to talk to my fist."

"Mmm," she purred in his ear. "Talk tough again. It makes me hot." She nipped his lobe, and desire shot through him.

Screw talking. He placed his hands on her waist and picked her up then placed her on his desk. She helped him sweep the papers off it as he lay her down. After pushing up her skirt, he dropped his pants far enough to expose his erection. Legs wrapped around his waist, she drew him into her body, a warm, wet haven he never tired of.

"Harder," she begged.

She wanted tough, he'd show her tough. He pounded into her body, hips pistoning while she cried out, but even as he let himself ride the wave of pleasure their quick coupling brought, he couldn't quite forget the battle he was going to provoke. And win.

Chapter Eleven

The guys no sooner made their phone calls than they were piling out of the motel into the truck. Thea could tell by the glower on Trent's face he wasn't happy. Not daring to ask why, she listened avidly when someone else did.

"What did he say?" Marc asked, his eyes trained on the road as he drove.

"He'll help us to a certain extent."

"Okay. What part is he balking at? Asking the other vamps for help? Gathering a posse to take Roderick out once we figure out how? Dangling himself as bait?"

"No. He agreed to all that so long as we can get the information we need from the vampires."

"Then what did he say no to?"

Trent clamped his lips shut, and Thea suddenly knew. "He doesn't want me at his compound."

He shook his head.

"That's bullshit," Marc exclaimed.

"What the hell?" Darren growled. "Don't tell me they're afraid of one little pregnant woman?"

Even though she was curled into Trent's side, she couldn't help a spurt of warmth at the *little* comment.

"They are," Trent admitted. "He was really

apologetic, but he says, given her close experience with the vamp, she's too much of a risk to bring into the pack."

"He is right," Jaxon added. "Little cutie pie over here might look like she'd only hurt a fly, but if Roderick's planted a bomb in her head, she could go psycho and cause all kind of damage."

"You agree with him?"

"No, but I understand. It's why I wanted Bailey to leave," Jaxon admitted.

"And?"

"She blackmailed me!" Jaxon sounded part shocked, part amused.

"What does she want?"

"She won't agree to leave unless she sees me."

Trent frowned. "But you're banned from the pack. How does she expect you to do that?"

"Once we get close enough, I'm supposed to call her and arrange to meet in a public place so her other mates don't kill me."

"Will you?"

"I shouldn't."

"But you will," Thea said. "She wants to see you, and I know you want to see her. What can it hurt?"

"Everyone," Jaxon growled.

"But you're her mate. Don't you owe it to her?"

"I owe it to her to keep her safe."

"And if she won't leave because you won't

meet her, then aren't you failing at that?" Marc interjected. "Sorry, dude. But didn't you tell me she was pregnant? Which makes her an emotional write-off. You better do what she says."

"Maybe. Now, how about instead of worrying about my personal problems, we focus on yours. What are we going to do with Thea?"

Too many sets of eyes fixated on her. She diverted their attention. "Forget me. I'd like to know instead what exactly you're planning to do that is so dangerous I can't come along."

An uncomfortable silence fell. "Well? I'm waiting," she said.

Darren cleared his throat. "Um, it's like this . . . Uh, you see . . ."

"Keep in mind we came up with this plan last night just after you went to sleep."

"What plan?" She narrowed her gaze on her lover, and Trent met her eyes, barely.

"We get you somewhere safe then use Jaxon's internal vampire GPS to find Roderick and keep tracking him while Nathan meets with the vampires and finds out how to kill him."

"And then you use this info, charge in like heroes, and save the day?"

Jaxon winced. "Ooh, dudes, when she puts it like that . . ."

"It sounds crazy," she said quietly. "You know, since you're so suicidal, I wonder why you didn't just plan to meet the vampires yourself."

Trent shifted in his seat.

"Oh my God, you did? So what made you give up that part of your brilliant plan?"

"When did she get so bossy?" Marc whispered to Jaxon.

"I heard that. You rescued me on a bad day. Today I feel great. Or did," she said with a pointed stare at Trent.

"I told you we decided this before it happened."

"And should have mentioned it before we did, you know." She clamped her lips tight and tried not to blush in remembrance.

"You're right. I should have. But that's the only plan we have for the moment, so unless you have something better . . ."

She slumped, suddenly deflated. "No. But I still think your plan is crazy."

Trent cupped her cheek and turned her head so she faced him. "Sorry, beautiful." He brushed her lips, a quick kiss that still created a flicker of heat.

"We all are," Darren said from the other side, leaning over the seat to rub her arm. It should have made her claustrophobic having two big males overshadowing her or at least uncomfortable, given she'd slept with one and not the other. But she found it comforting instead. Actually craved it.

"Oh, gag me with a spoon," Jaxon chided from the front. "Can you keep the foreplay to the privacy of your room?"

Thea blushed. Growling, Darren leaned forward and smacked Jaxon in the back of the head.

The male laughed. "Damn, if that doesn't remind me of my days in the pack."

While Darren bantered with Jaxon, Marc joining in as he drove, Trent pulled her onto his lap and put his lips against her ear. "I'll keep you safe. No matter what. And we'll make him pay for hurting you. That I promise."

But will his promise kill him? She knew firsthand what Roderick could do. Or had done to others.

As she lay nestled against Trent's chest, her mind whirred. She'd heard enough of Jaxon's story to know he thought himself immune to Roderick because he'd tasted the vampire's blood. *I drank some, too.*

Not willingly.

The memories came of when the monster fed from her wrist that first time while David watched and she'd thought she would die. A floodgate opened in her mind, and a passage of time she'd not realized she'd missed played in all its horrific detail.

It was early in her relationship with David. He'd brought home a bottle of booze.

"We should celebrate," he announced as he held up the tequila.

"What's the occasion?"

"It's been one week since you made me the happiest man alive." He followed up his claim with a kiss, but he pulled away when she tugged at his shirt.

"Not yet, hot stuff. First a toast." He wandered into the kitchen and sliced up a lemon, placing it on plate on the breakfast bar, along with the saltshaker and some shot glasses. He filled the small cups and handed her one.

"To us."

"To us," she repeated. The fiery liquid burned its way down while the lemon made her face screw up. Laughing at her expression, David then kissed her and insisted on another shot. And another. They drank—a lot. Most of the bottle, as a matter of fact, in between lovemaking. At one point, she passed out, and when she woke the next day, she couldn't move. And not because of her pounding head.

It took her a moment, for she was dizzy and sluggish, to realize she was tied to the bed. Panicked, she pulled at the restraints, but manacled by the wrist and ankle, she got nowhere.

"She's awake," someone said.

Startled, she turned her head to see a stranger sitting by her bedside. A scruffy-looking man who leered at her naked body.

"Oh my God. Help. Help me! David!" she screamed.

To her surprise, he walked in, his face an

expressionless mask. He flicked his gaze over her but said not a word. Shocked, she could only stare as he handed something to the stranger in the room. It turned out to be drugs. The other guy pressed a syringe in her arm, and although she fought it, blinking and cursing and straining, she slipped into sleep once again.

A sharp pain in her wrist jolted her awake. She tried to rear up, but the restraints still bound her hands and feet. Angling her head, she could see, even if she wished she didn't. A creature of nightmare, with sharp teeth and a wicked red gaze, loomed over her. His hands, tipped in claws, held her arm firmly, and she finally saw what made her wrist throb. The monster sucked at her flesh, each pull of his mouth draining her. Faintness made her shake, and she had to lay her head back down.

"Why?" she whispered. "Why are you doing this?"

Busy eating—*eating me*!—he didn't answer. Thea closed her eyes to the pain and the present, tried to bury reality under more pleasant thoughts. It didn't quite work, but weak from blood loss, she did drift numbly.

Until he forced her mouth open.

A warm, thick liquid gushed in, splashing over her teeth and tongue. She choked as her eyes flicked open. Horror caught her when she noted the source of the fluid. His arm gashed wide, the monster held her jaw open wide enough to catch the flowing blood.

Gurgling, her throat convulsing, she tried to spit it back. He growled something, and another hand, the nails dark with grime, appeared. It pinched her nostrils shut. Cut off from air, bound and unable to fight, as tears leaked from her eyes, she swallowed. And gasped for air, only to imbibe more as he forced it into her.

He did that for several days, eternities in her mind, before he seemed satisfied. Not that she remembered. She awoke one morning, oblivious. The missing days, a small worry that David smoothed over by claiming she had the flu. Then David distracted her by making love to her. Several times a day, as a matter of fact, until she got pregnant.

And everything changed.

But the true change occurred before that, she realized. The memory she'd recovered when Roderick bit her at the cabin made more sense now. He'd conditioned her somehow, managed to coax her wolf side awake using his own blood. It's what made the most sense. According to Trent, she needed to be part wolf to carry a baby of theirs. She just got pregnant before she could complete the change. Of more interest, it had taken Roderick's blood to transform her. *I drank his blood.* So if Jaxon's theory were true, the vampire couldn't control her with his mind. It made even more sense the more she thought about it. Roderick only ever hurt her physically, never mentally, not like he did with the wolves under his command. Knowing this, how did it help the situation?

She couldn't tell them she would be an asset because she was immune. She already knew they wouldn't accept her aid. They thought her fragile and weak. So she kept the knowledge to herself for now. It would come in handy later because she wasn't about to let them ditch her. An ability to fight Roderick could come in handy, if she came prepared.

"I need a weapon." Her sudden observation cut the conversation dead.

"What for?"

"Well, for one, while your wolves are pretty vicious and all, it takes too long for one-on-one fights, especially with the numbers we'll be facing. Isn't there a gun or something I can use to take some of his minions out?"

"Silver bullets to the brain work," Jaxon said.

"Then I want some."

"You?"

"I need to be able to defend myself."

"We'll protect you," Trent declared.

"What he said," Marc chimed in, and a "Ditto" came from Darren.

"Duh. I know that, but what if there's too many? Or they catch us by surprise? I should have something."

"She's right," Jaxon agreed. "So long as she doesn't shoot any of us, it's a good idea."

"Fine." Trent's agreement emerged with reluctance.

"And . . ."

"You want more? Perhaps my balls since you've emasculated us?" Trent growled.

She smiled. "Maybe later. No, I was going to say some clothes. No offense, but I need underwear and a bra. Deodorant would be nice, too."

As chuckles filled the truck, she inwardly smiled. She'd managed to convince them to give her a weapon. Now at least when the time came, she could at least fight.

When they finally stopped driving midafternoon while the sun still shone high in the sky, they rented two motel rooms once again. Only once they all piled out of the trucks did she stop to wonder at the sleeping arrangements. She was considered Trent's mate, but Darren had tried to stake a claim earlier that morning. She'd not missed either Marc's heated glances or kind gestures, like getting her some chocolate bars at the pit stop for gas along with a better-fitting T-shirt.

But she found Marc easy to ignore. Not so Darren, who stayed close by in the truck, his fingers occasionally dancing down her thigh, which made her hyperaware. She was thankful he never did it for long, just enough to make her heart patter a little faster.

And make her feel guilty she enjoyed it. *What*

is wrong with me? I'm involved with his friend. I don't regret sleeping with Trent and look forward to getting some alone time with him. But why, oh why, do I crave a taste of Darren? More than crave, she wanted to devour him. Kiss his lips until he panted. Claw his back as he plunged into her. And more shocking, she wanted Trent there, too. Watching, touching, showing her what he meant when he teased her the night before with his words of multiple lovers.

Was she ready though to toss everything she knew out the window, though? To believe him when he said women took multiple mates, without guilt or repercussions? To bind herself to another man for a lifetime?

She knew she couldn't make the first step. Didn't have the audacity to approach Darren, or even Trent, with her thoughts and desires. Perhaps she fretted over nothing. Just because Darren showed an interest didn't mean he would act upon it yet. After all, she'd just slept with his friend. Despite the kiss of that morning, it didn't mean Darren would try anything further. And she couldn't ask.

The answer to what would happen would have to wait a little longer, she surmised, as they opened only one motel door initially and everyone trooped in, flopping onto the two chairs, Jaxon on the dresser, Marc on the bed. Trent snagged her around the waist and placed her on his lap.

It seemed a blatant display of ownership, and yet, she allowed it. Enjoyed it, actually. No other boyfriend, including David, every displayed his interest that publicly.

"Okay, so we're going to need food. Clothes. Some toiletries."

"What about a doctor for Thea?" Darren added.

She shook her head. "I can wait a few more days. I'd rather get things settled with Roderick first."

Trent hugged her. "If you change your mind, let us know. As for the supply run, we obviously shouldn't all go. Too conspicuous. I'll stay here with Thea."

"Just you?" Darren shook his head. "We don't need three guys shopping at Walmart. Two will do. I'll stay as well."

"Why can't I?" Marc challenged.

"Because." A deep undertone seemed to coat Trent's words, and Marc, though unhappy, agreed with a sharp nod.

What was that about?

The moment passed, and Jaxon scrounged through the motel nightstand for paper and a pen. They made a list of items, and then Jaxon, with a wink in her direction, left with Marc while daylight still reigned.

Alone with the two men, nervousness suffused her, especially when she recalled her dirty musings of earlier.

"So what should we do while we wait?" Darren asked, his gaze trained on her.

She dropped her head and stared at the floor.

"I can think of several things I'd like to do." Trent's suggestive tone made her cheeks heat. Surely he didn't mean right at the moment with Darren still in the room.

Or did he? Her cheeks flushed with heat. "I think I'll go shower."

Almost running, she closeted herself in the bathroom, anxious and, at the same time, excited. Her heart pounded a mile a minute.

What had gotten into her? *More like who might get into me,* her mind snickered. She expected to sleep with Trent again, given the way he'd touched her all day long. The thing was she got the impression Darren planned to join. Or have a turn or something. She wasn't quite sure how it worked. Explaining to her that their kind mated in groups didn't exactly prepare a girl for what it entailed. And did she even want it?

They seemed to act as if it was a foregone conclusion she'd end up sleeping with all of them but Jaxon. That she would bind herself to them in a wolfish mating ceremony. Did she have a choice? It occurred to her to march out there and declare that she wasn't interested in being part of some group orgy. She didn't move. Couldn't, because it stunned her to realize it did intrigue her. Much more than it had when Trent told her about it. Something about spending the day snuggled against and surrounded by male bodies fired up her imagination and libido in a way she'd never imagined, but enjoyed.

Did she dare let herself live on the wild side? After what happened to her, did she truly want to live with any regrets? *I should at least give it a try.* That was if she'd read the situation correctly and the guys truly did intend to claim her.

She'd have to wait to find out now, though. She couldn't very well march back out still covered in the grime of travel and the previous night's traces of sex. With a sigh for running away like a coward, she turned on the water and stripped. After stepping into the tub, she tilted her head under the showerhead, letting the warm spray cascade over her.

Humming to herself, she soaped her body and rinsed. The rustle of the curtain didn't surprise her too much. She'd half hoped Trent would join her. His arms circled her from behind, and she leaned back into him, eyes closed as the water rolled down her length. He cupped her breasts, stroking his thumbs over her fat nipples, the callused touch making them pull into hard buds. The second rattle of the curtain rings on the bar startled her, and she opened her eyes to see Trent in front of her. So who was behind her? Could it be?

Craning her head, she caught a glimpse of Darren's blue-eyed gaze.

"What are you doing?" she asked breathlessly.

A stupid question, probably, given she had two naked men in a shower with her sporting obvious hard-ons.

"Logic says I should wait to claim you. Wait for you to be ready."

"But," Trent interjected, his hands skimming down her hips to tease her thighs, "with the way events are snowballing, why wait? You can feel he's meant to be with you, can't you, Thea?"

She wanted to refute his claim. Good girls didn't sleep with two guys. However, she'd always wondered if bad girls had more fun. She waited too long to answer while her mind mulled over the possibilities.

Taking control and making words unnecessary, Darren tilted her head to the side and leaned in to kiss her lips. Even with the awkward pose, a rush of excitement coursed through, an aroused tingle that increased as Trent pinned her nude body from the front. Meshed between two male bodies—slick, hot flesh sliding against hers in a sensual feast that roused her hunger—all her reasons for not allowing a threesome vanished. Who could think with two pairs of hands stroking down her body? A pair of lips claiming her own while the other tugged at her engorged nipple, sucking it like Darren sucked at her tongue? Quivers of pleasure made her moan and squirm under their touch. A hard cock pressed against her backside while she felt another, molten and thick, against her lower belly.

The shower proved crowded with the three of them, and with a growled "Bed!" from Trent, she found herself picked up, wrapped in a towel, and carried to a bed, all the while dazed and aroused as they continued to touch and kiss her.

Once she was on the bed, the towel was stripped off, and she regarded them through heavily lidded eyes. They stood at the foot of the bed, big, strong, and so very aroused. The sight of them, one so light, the other so dark, their expressions identical almost in intensity, made her hot. Hotter than hot. She needed. *Hungered.* The strength of her desire almost frightened, and for a moment, her morals tried to rear their head. "This is wrong," she murmured, a token protest even she didn't believe.

"Smells right to me," Darren said with a grin, kneeling between her legs.

"Looks great to me," Trent added, stroking his cock as he positioned himself beside her head.

Felt just right to her, she decided when Darren nipped at her thighs, his warm breath teasing her. Trent leaned forward and played with her breasts again, sucking and biting at her sensitive flesh. As for Thea, she could only thrash and gasp beneath their ministrations.

Darren moved closer to her sex, blowing across her damp lips, teasing her with a quick flick of his tongue.

"Lick her," Trent ordered. "Taste her sweet honey."

It should have appalled her, his explicit talk. Shame at the very least should have made her blush and want to hide, but knowing Trent watched . . . Oh God, it excited her, and she cried out as Darren lapped at her, his wet tongue swirling and rubbing across her clit.

"That's it, beautiful," Trent encouraged. "Wiggle those sweet hips of yours while you enjoy him tonguing you."

Such naughty commands. So freaking hot. She gasped as Darren groaned against her sex, the vibration making her channel clench in anticipation.

"Turn your head," Trent ordered.

Obeying, she opened her eyes as well and found him lying on his side, his hips angled so that his cock jutted before her lips. His fingers weaving through her hair, he urged her forward. "Suck me."

How dirty. Gone was the gentle, talkative lover of the night before, in his place a more commanding version, one who no longer held back. Who knew what he wanted. *And he wants me.*

She took his cock into her mouth, sliding her lips over his length, a moan rumbling over his taut flesh as Darren speared her with his fingers while sucking her clit.

Her orgasm took her by surprise, erupting

suddenly and pleasurably. Hands held her down when she would have arched off the bed. A cock muffled her cries as she tried to express herself. The waves of bliss hadn't died down when Darren shoved into her, his fat dick pressing against the pulsing walls of her channel. It felt so fucking good.

And then he started to pump.

* * * *

Darren wanted to piston hard and fast into Thea. He held back, which took a lot of self-control, especially with the way she looked: her cheeks flushed, her eyes glazed, and her mouth—*oh, fuck, her mouth*—sliding up and down Trent's cock, cheeks hollowed as she suctioned.

He held no interest in his friend sexually, but he couldn't deny a certain excitement at watching her pleasure the other man. Hands hoisting her thighs up, he averted his gaze to watch himself sinking into her soft flesh. Making love to her was like nothing he'd imagined or experienced. Each stroke was a slice of heaven, and he could feel his orgasm building fast. But she'd just come, so she'd need more if he wanted her to join him.

One arm braced over her legs to keep them up against his shoulders, he used his free hand to fondle her clit.

It must have caused quite the reaction because Trent hissed as he pulled his cock free of her mouth with a wet pop.

"Fuck. She clamped down."

Lost in pleasure, Thea didn't even react, just made mewling sounds as she clawed at the sheets.

"Move your hand," Trent said.

Darren did as told and wondered why until he saw his friend dip forward and start tonguing her clit. The decadence of it, along with warm breath, brushed him as Darren thrust into her.

"Bite her," Trent growled then moved away. "Take her as your mate now before she comes again."

"Thea?" Darren let a questioning note come into his one word.

She slid open her lids, her eyes glazed with passion.

"May I?" What a pussy way of asking. He should have just done it, but he wanted her permission. Wanted her.

She licked her lips. "Mate me, Darren."

"Are you sure?"

She answered with a smile that stole his breath. But where to bite? His gaze roamed her body, noting the old scar and fresh bite mark on each side of her neck. Breasts, belly . . . His roaming stare moved back up to her luscious tits. He'd found his spot.

Still buried balls-deep in her wet pussy, Darren kissed the creamy expanse, licked it, too, before he sank his teeth in. She cried out, arching, hard enough that he almost lost his grip. One thorough suck to taste her blood, and he released her.

"Come here." She gasped the request.

He quickly complied, and she grabbed his face and planted a fierce kiss on him before nipping his lip. The shockwave of their joining shook him, and he knew she felt it, too, because she screamed, her body tightened, and for a moment, she stopped breathing.

Darren couldn't help but whisper, "Holy fuck!" And then he was pistoning into her hard and fast. Her muscles milked him, and with her awareness—her pleasure, happiness, and more—rolling over him, it threw him over the edge. He yelled as he came, the moment of joining overwhelming and perfect.

Spent, he didn't protest when Trent tapped him, just moved aside as his friend took his place, pumping into her still-quivering sheath. She moaned, so lost in the aftershocks of her orgasm that she didn't even open her eyes.

With her legs draped wide, Trent fucked her, panting as he thrust. She could make only little breathy sounds, and Trent grunted, "Help her, she's right on the edge again."

Despite the proximity to a part he preferred not to touch, Darren shifted until his face was above her mound. This close, the smell of sex overpowered and drugged him. He didn't so much see Trent fucking her as he could feel it, sense it. Her legs already parted wide, it proved simple for him to lick her. Her swollen bud quivered at his touch, and Trent gasped.

"Fuck, I'm coming."

Darren sucked at her nub, pinching it with his lips, and she shattered. He even felt it through their bond.

It blew him away.

Chapter Twelve

Marc wasn't stupid. He knew his buddies and Thea fucked while he ran errands with Jaxon. It kind of pissed him off. *Why couldn't I have been second? Hell, forget second, why couldn't I be first?*

Just as attracted to Thea as his friends, his wolf just as eager to mark and claim, why was he forced to wait? *I should have done or said something.* Fighting, though, would have frightened her, so despite his disgruntlement, he went along. But he didn't like it. Especially not once he saw the soft looks and sated glow surrounding the three of them. As for the smell of sex, it still permeated the room, despite the fact that they'd showered.

Not showing his annoyance—and, yes, his hurt, dammit—proved hard as he spilled his purchases on the bed. A part of him wanted to yell. Hit something. Or, even better, fuck her until he could also wear the same stupid look of satisfaction. He did nothing, knowing any of those actions would get his ass kicked six ways from Sunday.

The hug she gave him, thanks for the clothing he'd bought her, went a long way to restoring his usual good humor. It seemed he wasn't immune to jealousy. He'd better get over it, though, if he hoped to join the others in mating. Thea already had her required two. Acquiring a third was completely up to her at this point.

Flopping on a bed, Marc ate along with everyone else, but Jaxon.

Despite the hours they'd driven, Jaxon paced uneasily. "I think we're going to have trouble tonight."

Yeah, the blue-balled kind.

"Can you feel the vampire?" Trent frowned as he asked. "I thought he couldn't travel during daylight, and night hasn't quite fallen."

A shrug lifted Jaxon's shoulders. He turned to peer out the window before answering. "He can't move around on his own, from what I understand, but his minions could manage it, I suppose."

"They could have him in a box inside a truck or something," Thea volunteered from her spot on the second bed, a solo seat she'd chosen with blushing cheeks after evading two sets of grasping hands. At least she possessed the decency to not shove her new status in Marc's face.

"But how did they follow us?" Darren asked. "We really covered out tracks this time, and once again, we parked a few miles away."

"Maybe Jaxon's sixth sense works two ways."

The man in question turned from the window with a sigh. "I guess it's possible. It just seems strange because Roderick never took my blood."

Thea turned gray, and Marc jumped in. "Hey, you're upsetting the pregnant lady, and she needs to eat. Let's change the subject before the food gets cold."

Thea's smile of gratitude was wan, but Marc clutched it like a prize and grinned back. He unobtrusively stuck up his middle finger at Darren, who glared at him as he moved to stand by the side of her bed. Trent only smirked. Funny how the bossiest of the three of them seemed to have the least amount of issues with sharing.

"Hey, Jaxon, seeing as how we're going to hit pack territory tomorrow, have you given any thought as to how you're going to meet your lady?" Thea asked seemingly unaware of the undercurrents peppering the room.

"No. I still think it's a bad idea."

"Jaxon, you have to see her. You promised." Thea sounded appalled.

"I know I promised, but I also made a vow to keep her safe, and somehow meeting with her kind of messes with that."

"What's the worst that can happen?" Trent asked.

"Hmm, let me count the things that could go wrong. One, she could get snatched. Two, she could get hurt. And while those are the two off the top of my head, they're enough to let me know it's a bad idea."

"You forgot you could get killed by her

mates, or have they forgiven you?" Darren tossed in.

A grimace twisted Jaxon's features. "No. They've not forgiven me. I just don't count my possible demise as a bad thing. She'd be better off without me."

"That's not true," Thea exclaimed.

However, Marc, watching and listening, had to wonder. If he knew he posed a danger to his mate, what would he do? Would he have the balls needed to stay away?

He hoped to never find out.

When his turn to watch with Trent arrived, he took himself outside, had to because listening to Darren make love to Thea, even from the next room, was making him antsy. A part of him understood that they didn't do it on purpose to make him jealous. He also knew that it was too soon for him to stake a claim. Things had already moved too fast, and Thea, given her human upbringing, could revolt all too easily. It didn't make waiting any easier.

Sitting up on the roof, watching the shadows for movement, he couldn't stop the whispers, the doubt from creeping in.

She'll never give me a chance now that she's so busy with Darren and Trent.

But she liked him; he knew she did by her smiles.

What use does she have for the weakest of the three? You know you're not as strong as Darren and Trent.

Hell, Darren could have ruled his own pack if he wanted to. His strength is why he's Trent's number two while I'm only number three because of friendship. Because other than that, he rated in the middle when it came to a commanding presence. Most of the time it didn't bother him, but now, with him shut out of the mated circle they'd formed with Thea, resentment bubbled. It didn't matter how big he got with his protein shakes or how much he worked out, something about him just wasn't as strong. As domineering. As attractive. *I'm just not good enough.*

What did he have to offer Thea? What could he give her that the others couldn't? Why would she want him when his only claim to fame was his friendship to a pair of alphas?

The litany of doubt wouldn't stop, and Marc alternated between depression and anger. *How dare they not give me my chance? She's my mate, too.*

Riled up, he almost jumped off the roof to go storming in to take what also belonged to him. To stake his claim on her flesh. But his inner voice stopped him. *Wait. Soon. Very soon. When the time is right, we'll claim her, and then no one will be able to keep us apart. And if they try . . .*

Recoiling violently from his next thought, Marc struggled to keep his balance on the roof. However, once whispered, even in his mind, the words wouldn't go away. *If they stand in our way, we'll kill them.*

* * * *

The plan to contact the vamps worked better than expected. By sunset, on the day the ad emerged in several print publications around the country, Nathan's new disposable cell phone rang. For like the thousandth time.

"If you're thinking of fucking with me," Nathan snarled in the receiver, "then hang up now before I come through this phone line and shove your head where the sun will never kiss it again."

"Seeing as how the sun hasn't kissed me in centuries, I don't see the point of your threat, dog."

The cool humor and fluid tones made Nathan tense. "Who is this?"

"Wouldn't the better question be, what am I? Although given your rather public and gauche attempt at contact, I would assume you already know."

"You're a vampire."

"Give a treat to the dog."

"I didn't place the ad so you could call and insult me," Nathan growled.

"Really? I'm sorry. Perhaps I should skip right to the point and kill you for being such a fucking idiot."

Nathan blinked as the speaker's tone turned harsh and commanding, enough to make him pause before replying. "Excuse me?"

"While we can easily handle the trite media portrayals of our kind, glittering like diamonds indeed, it is quite another for you to post an open challenge in the public where humans can see it."

If you like to drink blood and avoid sunlight then we need to talk. Don't make us hunt you down.

"Oh, please. They all think it's some big fucking joke. Trust me. I've been the one taking the calls. Your secret is still safe. That is if you are who you say you are."

"Ah, the dog shows some sense. You do well to doubt. But I assure you I am the real thing."

"Prove it."

Again, the low chuckle sounded, and Nathan resisted an urge to fling the phone across the room. "You mean the fact I know you're a Lycan isn't enough? What if I say the name Roderick? He is why you're calling, isn't he? Does someone miss his daddy?"

The mocking tone didn't help his frayed temper. "Rotten fucking undead bastard."

"My, my. What foul language."

"What did you expect considering you turned my father into a bloody monster?" Then again, his father hadn't exactly been a prize before his turning. Sentenced for crimes against the pack, Roderick and his broken mind should have died those many years ago. Instead, a sick man had been turned into an even sicker vampire.

"Yes, that was quite unexpected. And

unfortunate for the queen." The speaker's tone seemed to imply, however, that it was anything but.

"That's all you've got to say? It was unexpected? How about cleaning up the fucking mess you guys created? Roderick's been causing havoc for years now. Killing my people. Making them do horrible things." *Scaring me, not out of fear for my safety but that of my family. Totally unacceptable.*

"And your point would be?"

"Fix it."

"Why?"

The question emerged sounding so sincere that Nathan couldn't speak for a moment. "What do you mean why? Because he's a vampire, that's why. And a fucking psycho. Don't you guys have some kind of laws or police to deal with his kind of out-of-control behavior?"

"Yes, but again, why should we get involved? According to our sources, he's restricted his actions to Lycans. Why should we care if he rids the world of some flea-bitten curs?"

"You should care because he's not just hunting us. He's hunting humans." Nathan left out the part about them being dormant Lycans. The guy he spoke to didn't seem too sympathetic to his kind.

"Are you sure?"

"Oh, yes. Humans girls, actually. I can send you the news clippings if you'd like. He's doing things to them while pregnant, which I'm sure the media will love once they get their hands on this story."

"As if anyone will believe a tale of a vampire torturing women," the vampire scoffed. "They'll call him a serial killer, one who will move on with no one the wiser."

"How can you be so fucking nonchalant about this? Aren't you worried at all about what he's doing? One of his victims said he claimed he was making an army. An army for who do you think? He's already pretty much proven he can play with my kind pretty much at will. So who do you think he needs a rabid and loyal group of Lycans for? His own football team?"

"Excuse me a moment."

A click sounded in his ear, but the line stayed open and silent. Nathan drummed his fingers on his desktop. The vampire returned.

"What do you wish from us?"

Nathan didn't sigh in relief, even if some of his tension eased. For a moment, he'd worried he couldn't convince the blood drinkers to help him. "Tell us how to kill him."

A dark chuckle made him clench the phone tight. "Just that? Haven't you read the legends?"

"Holy water and crosses are for the movies. We can't get close enough to him for a stake or decapitation, and we don't know if sunlight will harm or kill him because we can't seem to find him during the day."

"So how does knowledge on killing our kind

help you if you can't find him?"

"Because we've got bait. We can draw him out." Or so he hoped. "But it does us no good if we can't finish him off."

A murmur too indistinct to make out made the vampire pause before answering.

"You've already got the right idea. Decapitation, followed by fire or sunlight. We regenerate rapidly, and with his Lycan heritage, Roderick even more so."

"What about a stake to the heart?"

Again the chilling chuckle echoed through the earpiece. "Legend. Actually, even decapitation won't truly kill us. You need fire to dull the vampire's abilities and keep him too busy regenerating, making it impossible for him to call his minions. Then, even if you think he's dead, you need to place him in direct sunlight for several hours. The UV rays will destroy any living particles left, and your vampire will stay dead."

"Fuck. If you guys are so damned hard to kill, how come you're not more in evidence?" Or running the country. Seriously, with that kind of almost immortal status, why remain hidden?"

"Humans are prolific and superstitious. Not to mention, we are not as easy to create as the media portrays. Our numbers are small, and we like it that way."

"Thank you for your help."

"Oh, this information isn't without cost."

"Excuse me?"

"Did you really think we'd hand over that kind of knowledge and not expect something in return?"

"Considering we're the ones who are gonna clean up your mess, don't you owe us?"

"Ah, but you're the one who has issues with Roderick. To us, he is family. A crazy member, perhaps, but still one of us. As such, you will owe us a favor."

"I don't think—"

The line went dead in his ear. Calling back proved impossible, as the number was unknown. Cursing, Nathan threw the phone at the wall.

What the fuck does that bloodsucker want? Nathan feared the answer but consoled himself with the fact that at least now they knew for sure what would work. If only it didn't seem so impossible.

Chapter Thirteen

Talk about a passion-filled night. Thea woke in the morning alone, but by stretching her senses just a tiny bit, the familiar sensation of Darren and Trent tickled her and let her know they'd not gone too far.

This new ability and what it meant should have freaked her out. Instead, it made her smile. A closeness like she'd never imagined existed between her and the men. And not just because of the sex, which was unbelievably explosive. No, the warmth she felt went beyond the physical. She trusted them. Knew on a level that transcended her gut instinct they wouldn't hurt her. That they truly cared for her and wanted only to see her happy.

A heady feeling for a girl who'd not so long ago thought she would die horribly or, worse, live a life of pain and misery.

She'd not said the *L*-word to them yet, though, despite her burgeoning feelings. She didn't really have to because she knew they felt her emotions too. Why did she hold back? She'd committed herself to them and, despite the short courtship, already felt as if she knew them better than she'd ever known David or anyone else.

So what am I waiting for? For them to declare

themselves first? Hadn't they shown their affection in the way they worshipped her body? Darren with his passionate lovemaking, his bright blue eyes boring into hers as he stroked into her hard and deep, crying her name as he came into her, her own body climaxing along with his. How about Trent?, Did he not prove it when he slid into bed in the middle of the night, his hands waking her with sensual caresses, his mouth hot on her neck, his lovemaking slow and languorous, leading into a climax that made her see stars? Did they both not prove it with gentle promises of protection, their care of her, the smiles that lit up their whole faces for her and her alone?

A knock on the door, followed by Marc's grin and tousled red hair peeking around the edge, brought her musings short. An automatic smile graced her lips, and yet, something had changed. For the first time since they'd met, she didn't feel a thing in his presence. Not even a teensy tiny tingle.

Modesty saw her gathering the sheet tight to her body, and that simple action caused a shadow to cross his expression. A shiver went through her as she wondered at his reaction and at her lack of one. Initially, Trent seemed to think, and she couldn't have disagreed, that Marc would also claim her as mate. Her inner voice seemed more or less certain of it as well. But mated already to two men, the tug she'd previously felt toward her third rescuer had disappeared.

It seemed she was content with two men in her life, which was already one more than she'd expected to settle down with. She just hoped that Marc wasn't too upset and that it wouldn't affect his friendship with Trent and Darren.

"Morning. I brought you some coffee," he said as he held up a steaming cup.

"Thank you," she replied, one hand holding the sheet snugly over her breasts while reaching with the other.

She didn't miss the flick of his gaze at her covered torso, a look that still stripped her bare and made her cheeks flush, but not in heat. Self-consciousness about her lack of clothing made her uncomfortable. A first since she'd met them. Perhaps, she'd not lost all her morals after all. "Where are Trent and Darren?"

Again, a shadow crossed his features, and his lips tightened—in anger or disappointment? She couldn't really tell before he turned away.

"Darren's grabbing some grub, and Trent's hashing over the plan with Jaxon for him to meet his mate."

"So he's going to do it?"

"Jaxon's not happy about it, but he is. He wants Bailey out of here before the shit hits the fan. But he's got to meet her in a way that won't have her other mates lining up to rip his head off."

"Lycans are a violent bunch," she stated.

"Very," he replied in a flat tone.

While he didn't look at her when he said that single word, she couldn't help a shiver. What was wrong with him today? Or was it her? Paranoia, the bane of anyone's existence. "So what's my role during this secret rendezvous?"

"You, beautiful, will stay out of harm's way," Trent answered as he strode into the room with a pair of steaming cups. "I brought you coffee."

She held up the cup Marc brought her. "Too late. Marc beat you to it."

A frown creased Trent's forehead as he eyed his friend. Marc shrugged. "You seemed busy, and Darren was gone. I thought she might like some while it was still fresh."

Before Trent could say anything, Darren entered with a box of doughnuts. "Breakfast of champions," he announced, holding it up.

Trying to keep ahold of her sheet while eating a powdery doughnut proved interesting, especially when Darren flanked her on one side and placed an arm around her possessively. She leaned into him, trying to ignore how Marc's nostrils flared.

Why, oh why did she feel so uncomfortable around him now? Had the mating with Darren changed her so much? Because she'd not felt like this after joining with Trent.

As if sensing her discomfort—actually they probably did through their bond—Trent led Marc to the door on the pretext of asking him to grab some more coffee. He flicked on the television and turned up the volume.

Connecting door shut, alone with her two men, her shoulders slumped.

"What's wrong, honey?" Darren asked, tipping her chin up.

She chewed her lower lip. "Nothing."

Trent seated himself on her other side. "We can tell you're lying. Did something happen? You can tell us. No one will hear."

"Yes. No. Kind of." She flicked a glance between them then dropped it to stare at her half-eaten doughnut still clutched in her hand. Avoiding the real question, she posed a sidestepping one. "Do I have to take another mate?"

"No." Trent drew out the word. "Pack law states a minimum of two, which you already have. A better question is, why are you asking?"

"Because."

"Thea," Trent said in a warning tone.

"I don't think I can handle another guy, okay?"

"That's not the full truth," Darren stated quietly.

"What's the matter, Thea? I thought you felt a spark for Marc."

"I did. But it's gone."

"Gone?" Darren repeated. "Are you sure it was there to start with?"

She nodded. "Yes, but not as strong as I felt

with you two. But when he came in this morning, it wasn't there anymore. I—I don't think I want him to claim me as a mate."

"Then you don't have to," Trent said soothingly. "The choice is yours, Thea. No one is going to force you to mate him."

"You're not mad?"

"Why would we be mad?" Darren asked, his hand tugging down the sheet, exposing her breasts.

"Because he's your friend, and I get the impression he kind of liked me."

On her other side, Trent's hand continued to pull the sheet down, skimming over her bare skin as it emerged. "Quite honestly, while I did think he'd end up part of any mating group I was in, I'm also just as happy to not have to share you with another."

"Ditto what he said," Darren added, sliding himself down along her legs until he could crouch between them.

"But—"

"Shhh," Trent murmured, turning her head so he could slide his mouth against hers. "No more worrying. We have a few hours before we need to go anywhere, and I, for one, know what I'd like to do with that time."

Kissing his way up her thigh, an act that both tickled and aroused, Darren didn't need to reply to show what he preferred to do.

Caught between them and happy about it,

Thea let her worry evaporate under their exploring hands and mouths. Trent possessed her mouth while his hands cupped and squeezed her breasts, his thumbs rubbing over already erect peaks.

Darren, oh my goodness, Darren, he blew softly on her sex, and she panted in anticipation, knowing what was coming, wanting it desperately. But he kept teasing her instead, circling his tongue and mouth around the part that ached. She grabbed his hair, tugging at him in a silent plea to give her what she needed. His warm chuckle drifted across her pussy, and she shuddered.

"I think she needs something," Darren said, blowing each word across her moist flesh.

"Then we should give it to her." Big hands grasped her and lifted. With a shuffle of bodies, Trent positioned himself in her spot, his back against the headboard while she knelt over him facing outward, her cleft hovering over his cock. Darren, now between Trent's legs, gazed up at her with smoldering eyes.

"Sit on his dick, honey. I want to watch that sweet pussy of yours taking him in, inch by inch."

Oh, how his dirty words excited her, almost as much as his ardent expression. She would have impaled herself on Trent right then and there if he hadn't still had a hold of her waist. He slowed her descent onto his prick, letting her feel his thick head parting her lips, making her tremble as he slid into her, agonizingly slow, stretching her around his length while Darren watched in rapt fascination.

Slowly, but pleasurably, Trent kept lowering her until she sheathed him completely. Legs draped alongside his, seated in his lap, she leaned back against his chest, her head tilting to let his lips find the shell of her ear.

"You feel so fucking good," he groaned, arching his hips to drive a little deeper.

Her breath caught.

"Bring those knees up," Darren growled. "I want you spread wide for me."

Doing as told, she bent her legs and opened them to expose herself before him. She should have felt embarrassment—the old her probably would have—but with her bond to the two men, all she suffered was anticipation and excitement. How could she not when she sensed how aroused they both were? How desirable they found her, even with her rounded tummy?

Darren crept closer, his big hands palming her spread thighs, holding her in place while he leaned in. His hot breath whispered over her throbbing clit.

"I'm going to lick you while you ride and make you come so fucking hard," he promised and then proceeded to perform, true to his word.

Thea could only go along for the ride, the climactic, heart-stopping, pulse-pounding ride of her life.

* * * *

A less secure male would have never allowed another man to get so close to his junk. Trent was anything but. And while he had no interest in Darren per se, he couldn't deny enjoying the hot breath tickling the base of his shaft as his best friend teased their mate.

Hands firmly gripped on her waist, Trent didn't move much, just pressed her down on his cock, letting her quivering muscles grip him sweetly while she cried out. Lips pressed to her neck, Trent watched as Darren lapped at her clit, his hands keeping her thighs spread wide as he licked. Thea's body tightened around him, her sex coiling itself, on the pinnacle of pleasure. Fuck, he loved how responsive she was. Loved everything about her from her bravery, despite what she'd been through, to her shyness when uncertain. He loved how joy lit her expression when she saw him and the way she teased him with words.

I love her.

He whispered this admission into her ear as he pushed her down hard on his cock. She shattered, instantly, crying out his name, her silky flesh milking him. But he held off, gritting his teeth, even as her sex sought to pull his climax from him.

While she still panted and lolled in his arms, Trent met Darren's gaze.

"Help me flip her onto her hands and knees." With two pairs of hands, it took them only seconds to reposition her so that her face was poised over his glistening cock while Darren knelt between her legs, his own shaft pointing.

"Beautiful," Trent murmured, "can you handle some more?"

Eyes glazed and lips swollen, she peeked up at him, and a smile to put all temptresses to shame tilted her lips. "Can you?" she purred before wrapping her lips around him.

Trent hissed as she took him in her mouth, hard and fast, grabbing him by the base as she did.

"God, she is so fucking hot," Darren exclaimed, fisting his shaft.

"Perfection," Trent agreed.

"Grab her by the hair," Darren said, his tone almost a guttural growl. "Make her bob for cock while I fuck her."

Some women would have recoiled at their dirty words and even naughtier act. Thea, oh, his sweet and beautiful Thea, she moaned instead and sucked faster. Harder. It felt so fucking great.

Trying to hold off a little bit longer, he watched as Darren rubbed his cock against her wet sex, and while he didn't have a direct view, he could imagine it from the way she groaned around his cock and her buttocks thrust back, begging for more.

She squealed around his length, a humming vibration that made his hips jerk, when Darren thrust into her, deep and hard. Even with the television blaring in the background, he could hear the fleshy smacks of his friend driving her with his shaft, plunging into that silky haven.

And she loved it. Head bouncing up and down without any urging from him, she suctioned his length while gripping the base of him tight. She grazed her teeth on his sensitive skin, sucked extra hard at his head, and when she plunged down, taking him as deep as she could down her throat, screaming as she came, he spurted. Hands wound tight in her hair, hips arched to sink even deeper into her mouth, he gave her what she wanted and shuddered as he watched her still getting it from behind.

Fingers sunk into her cheeks, pistoning fast and furious between her legs, Darren yelled when he came, his body bowing into a taut arc as he thrust one last time into her. A shudder went through her, and she moaned weakly, her breathing more a harsh pant.

For a moment they remained in their decadent tableaux, his semi-hard cock held limp between her lips, Darren slouched over her backside.

What a way to spend the morning, and even better, he'd spend the future doing this again and more. *Lucky me, amidst danger and chaos, I found the one person that makes me feel complete.*

And he'd kill to keep her safe.

* * * *

Jaxon eyed Marc as he paced the room. The man he'd gotten to know over the past week seemed different. Edgier. Angry. And Jaxon bet he could spell the reason: Thea.

His redheaded friend was jealous, and while Jaxon could sympathize—after all, Bailey never even claimed him until they were prisoners—he also knew it was a woman's choice. And women didn't like it when men got whiny or pissy about their affection.

"Wearing a hole in the carpet won't make you feel better," Jaxon announced.

"Who says I'm feeling bad?"

An arch of a brow was Jaxon's only reply.

A heavy sigh left Marc. "I don't know what the problem is. I thought I was fine with her taking her time. Getting to know me first before claiming me."

"But?"

"But how the hell is that supposed to happen if she's fucking Darren and Trent at every turn."

"If she's meant to be your mate, then she'll choose you."

"What the fuck is that supposed to mean? Are you trying to say I'm not?"

Belligerent and scowling, Marc faced him

with clenched fists. Jaxon's gaze narrowed. Was there something more at play than normal jealousy? Or had paranoia finally taken over? Was he doomed to believe everyone was a spy or puppet for Roderick? He'd hate to have to kill his new friend. And besides, Marc's mood swing was more than likely his frustration—a.k.a. blue balls—making him testy.

"I'm not saying anything other than to have a little patience and belief. Bailey was once like Thea. Actually, worse in a sense because she truly had no interest in mating with more than one male while your Thea at least seems inclined. Bailey allowed Gavin and Wyatt to claim her quickly, but her seduction of Parker took more time. And had I not betrayed her, according to her, my own claiming was imminent. Our polyamorous way of life is not an easy thing for women to accept, especially those who started human." Such a serious speech coming from him. Wyatt would have peered at the sky looking for pigs with wings if he'd heard it. Nothing like heartbreak and loneliness to make a man lose his sense of humor.

A heavy sigh and Marc's shoulders slumped. "I know. It's just harder than I expected, I guess."

"Wait until this whole mess is over with. You'll be able to go back home and woo her properly." Or so Jaxon hoped. Trent had spoken with Nathan this morning, and while they now knew what would kill Roderick, permanently this time, it didn't mean the task would prove easy. Actually, given the steps involved, the chances of success were slim. This wasn't the type of operation that could have too many people involved, or at least those weak of mind. As it was, Jaxon knew Marc would be a liability in their upcoming battle, his mental process not as strong as his friends. It's why they would task him with the job of guarding Thea. As for their battle with the monster, that would involve himself, Trent, Darren, Nathan as bait, and a few other strong-willed Lycans. They hoped to draw Roderick into a trap and, once they did, pray they could prevail.

But in case it all went to Hell, Jaxon wanted Bailey far, far away. Approaching the end of her pregnancy, she was vulnerable, and Jaxon wouldn't risk Roderick getting his claws on her.

Which was why he would give in to her demand to meet. Truthfully, a part of him thirsted for a sight of her. A whiff of her scent. It was more than he deserved, and a part of him knew his decision belonged in the Guinness book of bad ideas, but he couldn't help himself. Couldn't deny her, or himself, what would probably be their last chance to see each other.

Hours later, having slipped into the changing room of a chain store for maternity clothing in the mall, he waited, hoping Bailey would come to her senses and stay away. Desperately wishing she would show up early and put him out of his misery. Darren accompanied him, along with Marc, not in the store itself but in the shops just around it, backup in case the wrong sorts showed up. *Hey, wait a second, isn't that me?* His dark mirth failed to cheer him.

He heard her before he set eyes on her, the sweet sound of her voice making him shut his eyes.

"Oooh, look at these pretty dresses. What do you think, Wyatt?"

"I think they look like dresses," growled his former packmate, still as irritable as ever.

"Look who's Mr. Grumpy-pants today."

"I hate shopping."

"I know, but I'm tired of wearing the same thing all the time, and I need new underwear. Oh, and a bra."

"Why not shout it a little louder?" Wyatt said wryly.

"Well, excuse me for wanting to dress myself. You know you don't need to hover over me in the store," she remarked. "You could sit outside and wait for me if you're so uncomfortable."

"I'm guarding you."

"From what? Horrible floral prints that make my ass look wide?"

Jaxon couldn't help grinning as she said something the old him would have.

Wyatt growled.

"Lighten up, Wyatt. We're in the middle of the mall, surrounded by humans, during the day.

And you'll be sitting over there with the other guys, close enough to kick some ass if I yell."

"What if you can't yell?"

Jaxon could almost picture her indignant look. With a heavy sigh, Wyatt caved. "You win. Spend a ton of money, sunshine. But forget the underwear. You know I prefer you without." A giggle and the sounds of a kiss ensued.

After waiting what seemed like an eternity, but was in actuality only a few minutes, even expecting it, Jaxon jumped when cubicle eight at the far end of the row opened and Bailey stepped in.

At the sight of her, looking glorious, her hair still as wild and curly as he recalled, her face still his idea of perfection, all his strength left him, and he fell to his knees, tears in his eyes. He dropped his head, unable to look at her. Not deserving of it. To his horror, she dropped to her knees in front of him and cupped his cheeks.

"Jaxon," she whispered as she lifted his head. His blurry vision met her gaze, and suddenly nothing else mattered. Not the danger Roderick presented. Not the fact that Wyatt was close by and would kill him. Not even the fact that he didn't deserve her love. Everything got washed away by the love in her gaze, a love for him. Her lips trembled as her eyes filled with tears.

"Oh, Jaxon." She sighed his name before leaning in to kiss him.

Like a lightning strike, the simple touch

blasted through him, tore down his defenses, and laid him bare to her. He could feel the same connection, the same reaction emanating from her, and it shocked him like a bucket of ice-cold water.

If I can feel it, so can Wyatt.

He pulled back from her. "Sweet cheeks, we can't. We don't have time. Wyatt will get suspicious."

"He's always suspicious," she replied with a mischievous grin. "It's part of his charm."

"He'll feel your emotions seesawing through the bond."

"I'm pregnant," she reminded. "I seesaw a hundred times a day. Trust me, he won't panic unless he thinks I'm scared."

"You have an answer for everything," he said wryly, unable to help himself from rubbing her soft cheek.

She turned her head into his caress and kissed his palm. "I learned from the best." She wrinkled her nose and faced him. "What the hell is that perfume you're wearing? It's god-awful."

"But effective," he said with a smile. "It's some kind of cheap cologne."

"Did you bathe in it?"

"Almost. I call it eau of not getting my ass kicked before I save the girl."

Her smile faded. "You don't have to do anything. Actually, make that I don't want you to. Roderick is too dangerous."

"Which is why he needs to be stopped."

"You could get hurt."

"I can't walk away knowing you're in danger. I won't negotiate on this. And the showdown is coming, Bailey. Soon. Which is why you need to leave with the guys and hide. Don't let anyone know where you're going."

"I won't run like a coward," she stated, tilting her chin defiantly.

"It's not cowardly to protect yourself and the child." He let himself touch her and placed both his hands on her large stomach, the nudge of a foot against his palm startling him.

"I'm safer within the pack."

"I'm not convinced of that. Please, Bailey. For me. It's the last thing I'll ask of you."

"I hate this," she cried. "Hate the fact you can't come home. It wasn't your fault."

"Shhh," he urged, drawing her into his arms. "Please don't cry."

Clinging to him, she sobbed silently against his chest, her tears soaking the fabric and tearing his heart. Jaxon got no warning before the stall door was ripped open. A glowering Wyatt stood in the hall outside the changing room.

"You!" He spat the word, and his tone and expression conveyed his anger.

Bailey flung herself in front of Jaxon. "Don't you dare, Wyatt."

"Get out of the way, Bailey."

"No. You will not hurt him. I forbid it."

"Excuse me?" Wyatt's incredulous note probably matched Jaxon's face. If the situation weren't so fraught with tension, he probably would have laughed.

"You heard me. You will not lay a hand on him. He's here because I made him come."

"Made him?" Wyatt sputtered. "Have your hormones completely fucked with your mind? You met with the guy who handed you over to a monster."

"One, he's not just any guy. He's my fourth mate. And he also saved me."

"Which is why we didn't hunt him down and kill him," Wyatt growled.

"Thanks," Jaxon said drily. "I think."

"You," Wyatt snapped in his direction, "stay out of it."

"What the heck is going on?"

Jaxon wanted to groan as Parker appeared behind Wyatt. He'd thought it odd she seemed to have only one guard. He should have known better.

"You should have stayed away, brother," Parker rumbled, cracking his knuckles.

Undaunted, Bailey planted her hands on her hips. "Not you, too. For the last time, I made him meet me. He's my mate whether you all like it or not. And if I want to see him, I will."

"Not!" Wyatt growled.

"I knew this was a bad idea," Jaxon muttered. "Listen. I didn't want to cause trouble, but meeting her was the only way she'd agree to leave before the shit hits the fan."

"Leave? What shit? Bailey, what haven't you told us?"

"Excuse me," a hesitant female voice interrupted. "I don't know what you're doing, but could you do it elsewhere? You're scaring the patrons."

"I'm hungry," Bailey announced. "Let's go eat something, and Jaxon can tell you why he's here."

None of the men seemed to like the plan, but with Bailey's belly leading the way and no one daring to contradict their very pregnant mate, they all followed. Jaxon noted Darren and Marc trailing at a discreet distance.

Seated on an uncomfortable plastic chair in the food court, Jaxon brought them up to speed on everything that had happened. He stared at the table as he did so, unable to look his former brothers in the eyes, bolstered only by the fact that Bailey wouldn't let go of his hand.

At the end of it, silence reigned for several moments while his words sank in.

"Sooo," Wyatt drawled, "you're trying to tell me that sucking back the vamp's blood made you immune to his power."

Lifting his shoulders in a shrug, Jaxon replied, "It's the only theory that makes sense. I've come close to him about a dozen times now since we split. I've yet to feel him touching my mind or sending me to my knees crying for my mama to kill me."

"What makes you think sending Bailey away from the pack will protect her?" Parker asked.

"I don't know. All I know is I need Nathan's help to do this, him and anyone strong enough to withstand Roderick. But I also can't have that many strong minds leaving the pack alone and unprotected, so the showdown needs to happen close by."

"And what makes you think he'll come?" Wyatt asked as he drummed his fingers on the scarred plastic table.

"Roderick's gotten more erratic of late. Bolder. I think our last foray into his territory and our snatching of Thea from under his minions' noses pissed him off. I can feel him close by. Waiting for his chance. Nathan's been lying low, knowing how much his father hates him. He's agreed to let us use him as bait. When Roderick makes his move, we'll attack, and hopefully prevail. But if we don't . . ." Jaxon couldn't finish the sentence.

"If the plan backfires and all the strongest pack members are decimated, then the rest of the pack is fucked. Nice plan," Wyatt growled.

"Got a better one?" Jaxon snapped back. "Or are you content to sit back and watch our numbers dwindle? To run inside a fenced compound for the rest of your life? To have your child, my child, too, since I'm also her mate, grow up living in fear and hiding? I didn't take you for a coward."

Bold words thrown, Jaxon braced himself when Wyatt popped up from his seat, ready to clock him.

"Sit your ass down," Bailey commanded in a quiet tone. "You're drawing attention."

With a growl and eyes that promised a smack later, a later Jaxon planned to be far away from, Wyatt sat back down. Arms crossed and glowering, he kept his lips clamped shut.

Parker rubbed his chin. "Jaxon's plan, while dangerous, has merit. We've spent the last few months acting defensively. Bringing the smaller packs in to make ourselves stronger. Instituting martial law and curfews. While these things might bring some measure of defense, they won't solve the problem. It needs to be done. But I'm afraid I have to agree with Bailey: running is not a good idea."

The claim stunned him. "Not a good idea? But she'll be in danger if we fail."

"And if you take us out of the fighting equation, you're going to battle without some of the strongest fighters around," Parker explained.

"If his plan is real and not some ploy to get us all killed," Wyatt muttered.

"I believe him," Bailey stated.

"Good for you," Wyatt retorted.

"Actually, I do, too," Parker added. "The mating bond with him is weaker because they didn't consummate, but he's telling us the truth, and I don't sense any undertones that don't belong."

"We didn't last time either," Wyatt pointed out.

"Stop it," Bailey exclaimed. "He's trying to make things better. You could at least give him a chance. I know I want to."

Jaxon didn't like seeing her at odds with the mates she lived with. The ones who deserved her trust and affection. "I knew this was a bad idea. I should never have come. I'm sorry." He stood and looked away from Bailey's trembling lips.

"Jaxon. Please don't go. Please."

"I have to. Stay safe, sweet cheeks." Before he could walk away, she jumped up and hugged him. She squeezed him so tight that those blasted tears welled up again, and hugging her back, he couldn't wipe them away. And Wyatt saw his weakness.

Throat tight, unable to speak, he brushed a kiss on top of her head, pried her loose, and handed her to Parker. Then he did the hardest thing ever. As she sobbed, heartbroken, needing him, he walked away.

Chapter Fourteen

With nowhere safe to send Thea, they were forced to keep her with them as they waited for Roderick to show, an option Trent did not like at all. Jaxon claimed the monster approached, his strange bond to the creature an odd way of tracking for a wolf used to relying on his senses.

As her mates, it proved natural for Trent and Darren to take up permanent residence with Thea in one motel room, ensuring one always remained with her as they took turns on guard duty. While Marc never came out and asked or said anything about the arrangement, Trent could see him watching. He also noted his discontent but did nothing about it. With them all caught in such tight quarters, Trent thought it more prudent to say nothing, unsure of how Marc would react if told Thea showed no interest in taking him on as a mate.

Besides, perhaps it was the stress of the situation or the newness of her status making her say that. Perhaps once they returned home, the spark she felt before would return. If not, then at least, once Marc knew the truth, he'd have somewhere to go without having Thea's choice slapped in his face at every turn.

Trent refused to contemplate Jaxon's warning

that Marc might be under the influence of the vampire. *No fucking way.* His best friend was just reacting from the stress of the situation, a stress compounded by the fact the woman he wanted had yet to return his affection.

The coming battle had everyone on edge. The town that sprang up west of the compound grew taut with tension. Strangers were eyed with distrust and encouraged to leave. Many of the townsfolk knew of the Lycan secret, some of them dormants who chose to live outside the pack and provide what aid they could, taking up positions with the local law enforcement or running Lycan-friendly businesses like the motel where they stayed. The uneasiness could be felt everywhere as people hurried during the daytime, never alone, none straying after dark. Guests of the motel left, and new reservations were rejected as management did their best to keep innocent humans away. Trent and his companions might have gotten the shove-off, too, if Nathan weren't distantly related to Murray, the motel owner. Despite Murray's wishes, they were allowed to stay with the understanding that damages would come out of their financial pockets. *Assuming we survive the coming conflict.*

The uneasy waiting took its toll. Jaxon wandered around morose and wouldn't smile at all since his meeting with Bailey, a failed venture that saw her refusing to run to safety. The only good thing that emerged from it all was Trent's talks with Nathan, who assured him that, if Roderick could be dealt with, their rogue status would be revoked. One less thing to worry about for later.

With nothing to do other than wait and watch, he chose to discover his new mate. Her likes—watermelon, corny science-fiction flicks, and chocolate bars. Dislikes—spiders, broccoli, and spicy food. He brought her books on pregnancy and rubbed lotion into her burgeoning belly. The more he discovered about her, the more he loved her. It was a feeling he shared with Darren, who enjoyed making her laugh with his grand claims of the things he'd build for her. Between the two of them, they did their best to erase the fear that still came into her eyes when she thought no one watched. They did their utmost to make her feel loved, protected, and safe. It ended up a pleasant time of discovery, though rife with anxiety, which eventually had to end.

On their third day at the motel, just before the dawn, as he and Jaxon sat perched on the motel roof, his new friend said suddenly, "He's arrived."

But that was all he could tell Trent, the rising sun dissipating the link until nightfall.

It was enough. Knowing Roderick's wolves were around, possibly even closing in on him, didn't stop him and Darren both from loving Thea with a passion that left them all shaking and humbled.

I only hope it's not the last time.

Much later that day, after a flurry of phone calls and last-minute preparations, with a hard kiss to her lips, a kiss Darren matched, they marched off into the descending darkness. Jaxon's wry announcement of "It's a good day to die" caused a dark mirth.

Because it was. A good day for Roderick to die that was and for his vengeance to be complete. And so what if his fury had more to do with the abuse of his mate than his brother? In the end, the vampire's death was all that truly mattered.

As for Thea, left alone with Marc, who promised to guard her with his life, she wasn't completely helpless. With the help of the pack, Trent had acquired a small gun, one better suited for her hands than Jaxon's weapons, filled with silver bullets. He just hoped she didn't have to use it because, if she did, it meant they had failed.

Trent's confidence in their plan increased once he met up with Nathan and the thirty or so odd shifters he deemed strong enough to withstand the mind control,

"Nathan," he said, holding out his hand. The council leader shook it firmly, oozing the strength that made him alpha, not only over his own pack but also the council he ruled with an iron fist. But Trent was no weakling in the dominance department. He didn't bow his head to the other man, which earned him a wry grin.

"It's nice to see you again, Trent. And you as well, Darren. Jaxon." Nathan's tone lowered to an almost growl, which Jaxon accepted with a shrug and tight smile.

"Hey, big boss man. Bet you never thought you'd see me again."

"You mean, we hoped," Wyatt snapped, moving to join them. Parker gave his former packmate a nod while a blond fellow Trent assumed was Gavin gave Jaxon a thoughtful stare.

"No fighting." Nathan said it quietly, but Wyatt immediately stood down. "Jaxon, are you sure you can lead us to Roderick?"

"He's broadcasting loud and clear, which probably means he's up to no good and we should get moving."

"Let's go then."

Trusting in Jaxon, something his old pack still seemed leery of, they headed off on foot into the woods on the other side of town, miles from the pack itself and too far for his liking from Thea, their unsuspecting bait. He'd wanted to tell her about the small change in plan, but they couldn't risk her giving them away because, according to Jaxon, Roderick watched and knew of their plan via Marc.

On the one hand, Trent didn't believe it. His best friend would never betray them. But he also had to admit, given the stories he'd heard Thea tell about the mind control, that he worried about leaving her alone with Marc in case he was wrong. However, Nathan had a point when he said, "Me, Roderick wants to kill. But Thea? He wants her back."

So Trent and Darren kept their mouths shut, left their beloved mate in the dark, and headed off to the rendezvous point far from the motel. All necessary steps in order for Roderick to come out of hiding. They needed to lull him into a false sense of security and then spring their trap shut.

Trent hated it. Hated knowing his best friend since childhood might be possessed by a monster. Hated even believing it. Even more, though, he hated leaving his mate, knowing she courted danger, something he'd promised to protect her from. But Nathan was right. They wouldn't get a better shot.

And Roderick wants her alive, he reminded himself, which lent her protection of a sort, or so he prayed. He'd die if anything happened to her.

The night grew darker as the clouds covered even the faint brilliance of the stars. Not that he needed light to guide him. His eyesight adjusted enough to move silently through the trees. Along with his Lycan brothers, they ghosted through the woods, pretending they hunted, when in reality they lay in wait for a certain vampire to take the bait.

* * * *

Thea paced, anxiety making her unable to sit still while Marc lounged in a chair watching her. His silent brooding made her uneasy, but with more things to worry about than his annoyance over not being allowed to go with the guys, she ignored it.

It still pissed her off that Trent and Darren had left her behind with him as a babysitter. Didn't they know she wanted to help? That she wouldn't prove a liability? She'd finally admitted to Trent her immunity to the beast, the fact she'd also drank of his blood. His reply, "Don't care. You're staying here where I know you're safe." Didn't he know caveman declarations had gone out of style thousands of years ago? Although she did have to admit she found it kind of sexy. Not that she told him aloud. She didn't want him to think he could just go around giving orders—outside of the bedroom at any rate.

As a matter of fact, she planned on defying his decree and would have followed, but he'd left her a guard in the form of Marc, who stood in front of the door and refused to let her leave. Surprising given she could tell he wasn't happy at not getting a piece of the action, their feeble "Someone needs to guard Thea" an easy lie to spot. They all knew, even if no one dared say it aloud; Marc didn't have the right kind of strength to withstand Roderick. Hell, she wasn't sure Trent or Darren could either. The only examples she'd ever met of defiance all ended up succumbing in the end.

Which is why I need to get out of here and help them.

"Why haven't you chosen me?"

Marc's abrupt question startled her. "Excuse me?"

He regarded her from under hooded eyes. "I said, why haven't you chosen me? You had no problem falling into bed with Darren and Trent. My best friends. When is it my turn?"

"I don't think this is the time for this conversation," she said, stalling. The spark she'd initially felt for Marc had never reignited. As a matter of fact, having him around made her extremely uncomfortable.

"When will it be time, Thea? I've been more than patient while you've been fucking my friends. Gangbanging them like some two-bit whore. What's the big deal with letting me in on the action?" He stood as he spoke, and with his last sentence, he mimed thrusting his hips.

Ill at ease, she took a step back. "I don't feel for you the way you want me to. I'm sorry, Marc. But I'm not going to sleep with you."

"Don't feel for me?" he repeated in a falsetto. "Oh, that's priceless. As if you gave me a chance. But then again, it's not like you've had time. You've been so busy spreading your thighs. I think it's time you spread them for me. It's been a while since I've had the pleasure of banging your tight cunt. Although, given your recent activity, I wonder how snug it still is." Marc's voice deepened as he spoke, and terror rose up to claim her as a red pinprick appeared in his eyes.

"Roderick," she whispered.

"You remember me! Halle-fucking-lujah! Now that we've gotten that out of the way, be a good girl and strip, would you? I want the dog—what's his name again, Marc?—to claim your ass before you come back to join me. I know you've missed me." A wide smile stretched his lips, and she backed away as he approached.

"Leave him alone."

"Who? This mangy cur? But I rather like him. He had such dark thoughts swimming around in his troubled mind. I just helped bring them to the surface. You really should have claimed him before I did. It might have been enough to stop me from doing this." Marc pirouetted and did a little jig, the movements jerky and terrifying.

Stumbling onto the bed, she tried to hide her seeking hands from him. "You are sick!" she spat in disgust, terror giving way to anger as her fingers gripped cold metal. The gun. Hidden earlier under her pillow by Trent, who somehow foolishly thought she might actually sleep while events unfolded.

"I am not sick!" he yelled, practically frothing at the mouth, his eyes wide, red, and wild. "You will respect me. Or I will make you scream, baby or fucking not. You will learn to obey me."

Roderick, encased in Marc's body, lunged, and she screamed as she whipped the pistol out. He slammed into her, throwing her up against the wall, the gun she held pressed intimately between their bodies.

"Leave me alone, or I'll shoot."

"Do it. I dare you," he snarled. "Kill your lovers' best friend."

She hesitated, his words a horrifying realization. Shooting the body Roderick controlled meant hurting Marc. What would Trent and Darren think? Do?

As he ground himself against her, his erection hard, his leer frightening, the answer was clear.

Crack!

Chapter Fifteen

Trent loped on two legs along with the others, the clear scent of wolves, tinged with the unnaturalness he'd come to recognize, reaching his nose. The battle of good wolf against evil loomed, and he looked forward to putting the days of inaction and waiting behind him. Through his link to Thea, he felt her anxiety but no fear, and he wondered if they'd misread Marc's actions and words. Or Roderick's interest in Thea.

Surely if Roderick intended to make his move, he wouldn't have his wolves coming to meet them so far from the motel still. *Perhaps we misjudged Nathan's appeal to the creature after all.*

Movement in the trees had him tightening his grip on the gun he held. He'd opted to remain human in the coming fight, the long knife tucked through his belt, one of many scattered among their ranks in the hope one of them would get a chance to take out the vampire. But while he chose to remain on two legs, most of his companions were prepared to meet the enemy in their strongest shape, their wolf. Furry or not, though, he was ready to fight.

He took aim, but a grip on his arm saw him lowering his gun as he turned to see Jaxon wearing a grim face.

"He's not here."

"What do you mean he's not here?" Trent asked. "I can see his fucking minions. Or are you telling me those wolves over there belong to someone else?"

"Oh, they're his rogues all right, but Roderick's not here. He's been moving away ever since we began our approach."

"Away? But Nathan's with us, and the attack is about to start. Surely he wouldn't flee the battle?"

"Apparently we misjudged Roderick's interest in Nathan, and who says he's fleeing? We're not the only ones who can create a diversion. The question, though, is, who is his real target?" The fear in Jaxon's eyes made it clear to Trent that he thought Bailey, not Thea, was the one at risk. Another reason why they'd chosen a point more or less between the two locations.

"So which way is he heading? Toward the motel or the compound?"

Jaxon wrinkled his face, his eyes shutting in concentration. All around them the snarls of battle erupted as wolves, both sane and not, met in a furry clash of teeth and claws. Trent itched to join them. Nathan, the biggest beast of them all, tore a path through the attacking wolves. Lucky bastard was taking his frustration out on anything that moved.

Jaxon opened his eyes. "We need to go this

way."

Before Trent could even follow his pointing finger, a chill swept him, as his bond with Thea grew taut with fear. *My mate is in danger.*

"Thea!" Without thinking or waiting, Trent shifted, dropping clothes and his weapons in order to run. And he didn't race alone. He recognized Darren and Jaxon alongside him. The other three wolves who joined them were strangers, but given they didn't attack, he could only assume them friend rather than foe.

How could we have been so stupid? Their plan to leave her alone to draw Roderick out didn't seem so brilliant now with her terror coursing through their bond. *Dammit. This wouldn't have happened if Nathan hadn't refused to take her in.*

But Marc was there to guard her. The idea did not reassure, especially as he couldn't help thinking of his friend's behavior lately. The doubt Jaxon planted. He'd assumed Marc's attitude had to do with jealousy, but what if something else ailed Marc? Perhaps one of those ticking mental bombs Jaxon had warned them about. Jaxon made no bones that he thought Marc was a puppet and spy to the vampire, but Trent found it hard to believe his friend would betray him. Didn't want to believe it.

If he's laid a hand on her, friend or not, I will kill him. Pregnant and unable to defend herself, Thea was a sitting duck if Marc turned on her.

Their roundabout trail through the woods

had led them closer to the motel than Trent realized. Sprinting on four legs had also made the return trip quicker so that, instead of the hour they spent trekking, it was only fifteen minutes to return. Fifteen minutes too long in his mind. He'd lost the others on the mad dash, vaguely noting them veering off in the darkness, perhaps to deal with the eerie howls that seemed to trail them, a distraction he ignored.

Loping out into the dark parking lot, Trent slowed. Then stopped. Utter silence reigned. The very air stilled with anticipation. He cast an eye over the area, noting their SUV and a pair of other vehicles in the lot. The motel windows loomed darkly, even the one he shared with Thea.

A shift in the night breeze brought with it a familiar scent, the putrid stench of his prey. *Roderick is here.* Ready for the scrabble against the edges of his mind, Trent didn't flinch at the probing presence, but he did grimace, the second time no more pleasant than the first.

Arriving at his side, Darren shook his head, whipping it back and forth in an attempt to dislodge something that wasn't actually there. Trent could have told him not to bother. Snuffling and putting his head between his paws wouldn't erase the tendrils that kept grasping for a toehold into his mind.

Enough. He wouldn't let some undead freak control him. It was past time someone killed the boogeyman who'd fucked with his brother and hurt Thea. *I will be her hero and save her from the monster.*

Or he could just kill the fucking thing because he'd enjoy it.

Trent padded farther into the parking lot, Darren at his side. As for Jaxon?

There was no trace of the man or wolf. No matter. If Jaxon betrayed them, then he'd die. But somehow Trent didn't think he plotted against them. More likely he hid and waited for the moment he could help the most. Or so he hoped.

Trent, however, couldn't wait for an opportune moment to strike, not with Thea in danger. Inhaling the rancid odor of the vampire, he headed toward his motel room, trotting then running as the monster's smell got stronger and stronger. It disappeared a few feet away from the door.

What the fuck? Nose to the ground, he sniffed the pavement to the sidewalk but each time got the same result. Roderick had passed through here, and then his trail ended abruptly. A new track, however, consisting of blood droplets began. For a moment his heart stopped until a closer sniff revealed it wasn't Thea's. But he recognized it. *Marc is injured. But did his injuries result from his protection of Thea? Or had his friend turned traitor?*

Changing shapes took but a moment, and

then he was able to let himself into the room. The stink of blood washed over him, but again, it didn't belong to her. Intermixed with the coppery scent was that of a weapon recently fired. Thea defending herself against Marc if he read the clues correctly. Jaxon had been right. His friend had betrayed them.

Despite what his gut told him, he performed a quick search of the room, but of Thea there was no trace.

Racing back outside, he noted Darren angling off to the side, following the blood trail. Trent, though, was done chasing his fucking tail.

"Thea?" He called her name. Nothing answered him back. He tried again. "Thea! Marc! Where the hell are you?"

"Gone. Gone. Gone." The words whispered around him, mocking him and rousing his anger.

"Come out here and fight like a man." Trent offered the challenge, not expecting a reply. A prickling sensation saw him whirling.

A shadow dropped down from the roof of the motel, and a cold wave of something, not quite a wind, more like a heavy, chilled pressure, attempted to smother him. An eerie chuckle echoed around him. "But I am so much more than a man. Wolf. Vampire. I am powerful beyond the imaginings of your weak mind, puppy."

Trent taunted the shadow. "Says a coward who sends his minions to do the real work."

"I need no help to subdue you," boomed the creature. It cackled. "Oh, how you'd like for me to dance with you. To rend each other's flesh? To exchange primitive blows? Why waste time hurting a shell when I can cause so much more pain in other ways?"

The tenebrous touch on his mind turned sharp, like pointy-tipped blades, dozens of them, probing for a weakness. Trent gritted his teeth. "I won't fall victim to your tactics."

"That's what they all say just before the screaming starts."

And for a moment, Trent wondered if the creature spoke the truth as the pain turned excruciating. *Fuck that.* With a bellow of rage, Trent charged, only to be met by a snarling shape.

"Marc?"

His russet-haired friend bared his teeth and took a step toward him.

Trent didn't retreat, not when anxiety for Thea remained at the forefront, a fear for her well-being that made his rage even stronger. He cuffed his friend aside and kicked him when he could have sprung back at him. "Where's Thea? What have you done to her?"

"I? Nothing. Although I'd think you'd be a little more upset that the slut shot your poor friend here."

Trent didn't even spare Marc a glance where he paced at his new master's feet. "She must have had good reason."

A low chuckle rumbled from Roderick. "It seems you and your friend wore her out because she just wouldn't lie down and spread her legs like a good little bitch."

"If you've hurt her—"

"Oh, I intend to. And I think I'll make you watch. Won't that be a treat, puppy?"

"I'll kill you first." Trent lunged, only to find himself taken down by Marc, who jumped at him and used both his weight and momentum to his advantage. Holding the snapping jaws at bay took up all Trent's attention, and Roderick used his distraction to play his mind games again.

Little wolf, little wolf, let me come in. The mocking whisper rapped at the edges of his mind, prying at it with sharp, invisible fingers.

Things might have turned ugly had Darren not tackled the russet wolf, tumbling him off of Trent. Engaged in a battle of teeth and claws, they rolled away. After springing to his feet, Trent advanced on the vampire, who laughed.

And it was then that the wolves, eyes pinpricked with red, poured from the forest.

Shit.

Trent debated at that moment if he should run with the odds stacked so grandly against him. But he didn't know where Thea hid. He couldn't leave her or Darren behind. Which left him only one choice. Fight. Fight despite the incredibly stupid odds.

The furry wave advanced, their eyes glaring balefully, their lips peeled back to show sharp teeth. *This is going to hurt.*

An ululation suddenly rose in the night sky, a symphony of howls that grew in tenor. Trent grinned as Jaxon chose that moment to join the battle, leading Nathan and the others into the fray. Silver bullets whizzing, Nathan evened the odds and drew attention away from Trent and Darren, still the pair closest to the vampire, who, insanely enough, laughed.

"Enough of the games. Time for you to die," Trent snarled.

Charging in Roderick's direction, Trent saw the bullet that hit the creature in the back and burst through his chest, followed by one in his neck and then his leg. The last made the vampire stumble, and his face darkened in annoyance.

The pressure around them increased, almost thick enough to touch. Darren shifted shapes and knelt on the pavement, cursing. His face appeared strained.

For a moment, Trent wondered if his friend would succumb to the vampire's spell. Thea shattered the attempt. With a scream of a pissed-off woman who'd been screwed over one too many times, she came running from behind a vehicle, firing her little pistol at the monster until it clicked empty. It didn't stop her charge.

Stupid, brave, adorable idiot. Trent's heart almost stopped when the vampire batted her feeble attack aside and clasped her in his arms.

"Move, and she dies," Roderick snapped, a claw poised at her neck.

And that was when the bullet burst from the vampire's forehead in a gory, bloody mess.

With a whistling shriek, the creature let Thea go and rounded on Jaxon.

* * * *

Facing his nemesis after all this time was almost euphoric, even if the bullet in the creature's head pissed it off instead of incapacitating it.

"Hey, blood breath, would it have killed you to shower before coming out to play?" Jaxon taunted. He wanted the vampire to focus on him, giving Trent time to scoop up Thea and put her somewhere safe. Although true safety wouldn't happen until Roderick died.

"You!" Roderick spat the word, and Jaxon grinned.

"Yes, me. What's wrong, Roddy baby, don't know how to fight without the mind games? Let me remind you." The satisfying crunch of his fist meeting the monster's face was one he'd treasure for as long as he lived, which, judging by the vampire's fury, would probably be seconds. The fact that the creature laughed even though Jaxon had crushed his nose really wasn't a good sign.

"I don't need to control your mind to take

you down. I. Am. Stronger!" Roderick dove on him, pummeling him with his fists.

Jaxon did his best to turn away the blows, holding up his arms to block them, but forget landing any of his own. It was all he could do to stay upright.

A leg sweep later, one he never saw coming, and he landed on his back on the pavement. The vampire straddled his body and crouched over him.

"Gee, Roddy, I didn't know you swung that way."

"Let's see if you're still laughing once I tear your throat out."

Roderick's eyes glowed red as his lips split in a grin that revealed pointed fangs. And Jaxon waited to meet his maker. *I'm sorry, Bailey. I failed you again.*

"Good-bye, dog." Roderick opened his mouth wide, but before he could snack on him, a blade sliced through his neck and the vampire's head toppled sideways.

Sputtering and spitting out the blood that sprayed him, Jaxon nevertheless remembered his manners enough to say, "Thanks, Nathan."

"Oh, it was my pleasure," his former alpha said. "And long overdue."

Rolling to his feet, Jaxon caught the flare of a match and watched as it arced through the air to land on the crumpled body of the vampire.

It ignited like dry kindling, snapping and

popping, the acrid smoke billowing and making everyone cough. A wail went up, a chorus of them as the rogues broke off from the battle and ran in circles. Some shifted back to their human form and clawed at themselves, leaving bloody rivulets.

Without Roderick to guide them, the possessed wolves got back what was left of their minds. And for some it proved too much. Poor bastards. He didn't envy Nathan having to sort through that mess.

A sensation of danger prickled him, and he whirled to see Wyatt glaring at him, alongside Gavin and Parker.

"Hey, guys. Anyone in the mood to roast marshmallows?"

"Told you he was still a fucking idiot," Wyatt growled.

"An idiot who risked his life to save us all." Gavin sighed. "This still doesn't change what you did."

"I know. But at least now Bailey is safe. Take care of her for me, would you?" Jaxon's throat closed tight against the tears. Unwilling to let them see him cry—*I do have some pride left*—he shifted shapes and bounded away, ignoring Gavin's shouted, "Jaxon!"

There was nothing left to say. He'd done his part and given Bailey a future. The only thing he could give her. *I love you, sweet cheeks. Be happy.*

Chapter Sixteen

Thea clung to Trent, shaking still in fear. She'd thought herself frightened when Marc attacked her, forcing her to shoot him so she could get away. But that paled in comparison to the icy terror that gripped her when she saw Trent facing off against the monster. Without hesitation, she came out of hiding to shoot the vampire. Truth told, she enjoyed it, a payback for everything the bastard had done to her.

Her spurt of courage almost cost life. But thankfully, the good guys had prevailed, even if they were large and hairy and sported big teeth. She never did get to see Roderick's final moments because Trent refused to let her go. And when Darren joined them, hugging her from behind, the tears finally came.

We survived. Against the odds and hope, they'd won against the vampire. Defeated the bastard who'd hurt her and destroyed her life. *The monster who inadvertently helped me find true love and happiness.*

"Thea," Trent murmured her name. "What the fuck were you thinking attacking Roderick like that?"

"I had to. I couldn't watch you be killed. I love you."

"My beautiful mate." He claimed her lips in a

scorching kiss that stole her breath. "I love you, too. So much that if you ever do something that crazy again, I'll put you over my knee and spank you."

"While I watch." Darren chuckled in her ear, his breath tickling. "But seriously, honey, next time, when the bullets run out, move away from the bad guy, not at him."

"Says the man who dove into danger without pausing." She craned her head back. "I love you, Darren. And despite your promise of kinky retribution, actually because of it, I will probably do stupid things like protecting you if I think there's a need."

"Beautiful idiot," both her mates said at the same time but in a tone that conveyed their affection. She laughed with relief.

It was over. Truly over.

But not done. She ended up having to tell her side twice, once to her mates then again to Nathan, who stood with his arm looped around his wife, Dana. Of Marc there was not a sign. Actually, all the rogues had disappeared, those who could still move that was. While Nathan arranged teams to track them down and bring them in for questioning—and a mental evaluation—she watched the flames that still crackled over what remained of Roderick.

Caught between two male bodies, she asked, "Now what?"

"We go home."

"But first," Darren said, spinning her to face him, "a shower and some sleep."

They managed the shower but forget sleep. With two sets of hands roaming her body, under the guise of cleansing, arousal sprang forth. In a wet tangle of limbs, they ended up back in the bedroom, where she ordered them to both lie on their backs. Kneeling between them, naked, but no longer self-conscious—who would be when their desire shone so brightly?—she spoke in a low murmur.

"Just over a week ago, I waited to die. Each day I woke I lived in fear and prayed for help, even death, to save me from my nightmare. Then you both came into my life, and while you didn't ride big white horses, you came charging in anyway and rescued me. And my child," she said with a pointed look down at her swelling abdomen. "But you did more than save me from a madman. You showed me what true happiness, what real love felt like. Real love doesn't mean putting up with someone because you feel you have to or conforming to what society deems right and proper. Love is following my heart. Love is waking with a smile because I embrace the day. Love is being held in your arms while I sleep. I love you, both of you. And this might sound sick, but I'm glad Roderick found me because, if he hadn't, I might never have discovered what true love is."

"Thea." Trent knelt on the bed before her

and stroked her cheeks with his thumbs. "I promise to love you forever. To keep fear and the monsters that inspire them at bay. I promise to care for you and our child." He placed his hand over her stomach. "We're family."

"More than family," Darren added, joining them, his hand rubbing across the other side of her belly. "We're pack. A bond stronger than you can imagine. We would die to protect you. We will do our utmost to bring you joy. And, as my brother here said, we will love you forever."

"And ever." Tears moistened her eyes. "I think I'm going to cry."

"We can't have that," Trent said with a chuckle.

"Nope or we would be failing as your mates."

Gently, oh so gently, they lay her down, their hands touching her, turning her tears of joy, into cries of ecstasy. When they drove into her body, one at a time, hard and yet slow, they whispered in her ear their love for her. They showed her that, even after the darkest despair, there was always room for a second chance. A second chance for love and happiness and a happily ever after.

Chapter Seventeen

"How long are you going to watch it burn?" Dana asked.

The sun, now high in the sky, had turned the smoldering ruin of his father's corpse into ash, and still Nathan stared, unable to shake the fear that the monster would somehow return. Worried that his family was still in danger.

"Will it ever be truly over?" he asked. According to the vampire he'd spoken to, it took only a few hours of daylight to kill a vampire permanently. It had been over eight. Roderick was finally gone. He knew this, and yet he still couldn't move.

"Roderick's dead."

"But the wolves he abused are still alive. What am I going to do with them? They're no longer under the influence of a vampire, but the things they've done..."

A sigh left her. "I don't know what to tell you. You can't kill them all. Some, like Jaxon, redeemed themselves or never sank to the depraved heights some embraced. You'll have to judge them, case by case."

"And so the nightmare continues."

"But at least now there is an end in sight." She hugged him, forcing him to look away from the pyre into her eyes. "It's over, Nathan. And you're not alone. We'll help you with the rogues. John, Kody, Gavin, and the rest of them. You don't have to shoulder the burden alone."

"I know." He did. His pack brothers would do their utmost to aid him, but some things only an alpha could decide. The fate of those who'd inadvertently harmed was his to decide and, if found guilty, his duty to punish. But one thing hadn't changed. "I love you, Dana."

"I love you, too. Come home with me. He's dead. We've won. It's time to come home to your family."

For a moment, he resisted the pull of her hand, his gaze returning to the pile of ash marking the pavement.

A deep breath in, a straightening of his shoulders, and he finally managed to turn and walk away. It was over. His father was dead, and the pack could once again run free.

* * * *

The baby came early. Stressed and frightened, Bailey went into labor within an hour of her mates leaving to fight. Lucky for them, she held off birthing their child until they returned. It was a bloody battle that involved lots of screaming and cursing—by their sweet-tempered mate—but at the end of it, Gavin held their daughter aloft.

"She's perfect!" he announced.

Yet, despite her perfect features, ten toes and fingers, Bailey cried and cried. At a loss, Gavin drew Parker and Wyatt aside for a whispered conference.

"We have to do something. She should be smiling not crying."

"You better not be implying what I think you are," Wyatt growled.

"We need to bring back Jaxon."

"After what he did?"

"I'm not crazy about it either, but it's not about us anymore," Gavin snapped. "It's what she and the baby need that count. He's paid his dues. He suffered for his actions and, by having a hand in killing the vampire, redeemed himself."

"And don't forget. Bailey forgave him," Parker added.

"But what about Nathan?"

"Nathan has already said he can come back. He just hasn't had a chance to tell him."

Wyatt scowled. "But it was so nice and quiet without him bouncing all over."

"So you'd prefer to make our mate suffer instead?"

They all turned to stare at her as she stared into their child's wrinkled face, tears rolling down her cheeks.

Wyatt sighed. "Fine. But he gets diaper duty permanently I say."

And on that, they all agreed.

* * * *

A few hours after the birth, her mates disappeared all at once, leaving her alone with her precious bundle. She stroked her daughter's soft cheek, and the tears rolled anew.

Bailey didn't understand the sadness tugging at her. Roderick was dead. Jaxon was safe. Her baby girl was born. She should have been smiling from ear to ear. But something felt incomplete. Wrong. *I need Jaxon.* Seeing him again had made that so clear. She'd not stopped thinking of him since their meeting. Cried all the time despite what her other mates did to cheer her up. She didn't even smile when Wyatt wore a pink T-shirt that said, It's a Girl!

She needed Jaxon, and yet, despite the monster's death, she couldn't have him. *It's not fair!*

A sound at the door made her lift her head. Her breath caught. Standing with shadowed eyes and a wan smile was Jaxon. She carefully cradled the baby with one arm before opening the other wide in invitation.

It took him only two long strides before he hugged her.

"Oh my God. Jaxon. I can't believe you came." She couldn't help crying as she rained kisses on his face.

He kissed her back, chuckling. "I missed you,

too, sweet cheeks. Although if you keep crying, I am going to get in trouble. My arrival was supposed to stop the tears."

She paused. "Gavin and Parker did this?"

"Wyatt, too." Her shock must have shown. "I know. We'll have to check and see if hell froze over."

"How long can you stay?" she asked, cupping his cheek.

"How long do you want me?" he quipped.

"Forever."

"I was hoping you'd say that."

"But how? They made it pretty clear they never wanted you near me again, no matter how many things I threw at them."

"Apparently, you could have spared the chinaware. They just want you to be happy, and much as it annoys them, but delights me, it seems I'm needed for that."

"You most definitely are," she declared. "Now give me a proper kiss."

"As my sweet cheeks commands." He embraced her, and that easily, her heart grew light.

She sidled sideways to make room for him on the bed, and he climbed on. He cradled her with one arm under her head and stared at their daughter.

"I know we've yet to do the wild thing, but I still think she got my nose."

She laughed. "Funny. Because Wyatt and

Gavin said the same thing."

"What about Parker?"

"He says she got his feet."

They both winced and then laughed.

Gavin entered, followed by Wyatt and Parker. They ranged around her, a comforting circle of four men that eased the tiny knot she'd held inside since Jaxon's disappearance.

"Happy?" Gavin asked.

"Ecstatic. Thank you."

"No, thank you for loving us."

"And for letting us drink booby milk. And just so we're clear, I want to take mine from the source," Jaxon said with a leer.

Wyatt smacked him upside the head. "Idiot."

Bailey smiled. Now everything was just as it should be. Everyone she loved with her, a family, forever.

* * * *

The sun completed its journey across the sky and sank into the horizon, painting the asphalt in a brilliant wave of colors before giving way to twilight. Wind stirred the heavy ash pile on the ground, swirling it and yet not managing to disperse it.

The parking lot remained mostly vacant, only a few vehicles remained to mark the sparse occupants. And of those who stayed, none were watching.

From the shadows trotted a red-coated wolf. It paused in front of a door, where the stench of bleach had wiped a bloodstain away. But he doubted he would ever be able erase the memory of the wound. The shame.

Backing away, he sidled over to the pile of dust. An urge to sniff had him lowering his nose. He inhaled and immediately sneezed, particles of ash lifting and blinding him momentarily. Shaking his head, he sought to clear his senses, but while the dust drifted away, he could do nothing for his muddled mind that still roiled with the images of what he'd done. Ears pricked, he heard the sound of a vehicle approaching, and he darted into the shadowy edge of the woods and watched.

A dark sedan rolled up, its lights dark, its engine but a muted purr. It stopped alongside the now cold ash, and a door opened. Hands clad in black leather gloves emerged with a small broom and dustpan. A few brisk strokes was all it took to sweep up the remains and deposit them in a carved wooden box.

When all the ash had been moved from the pavement to the receptacle, the hands withdrew, the door closed, and the vehicle drove away. It disappeared into the shadows from whence it arrived with only a russet wolf, a traitor to his kind, as witness.

Epilogue

The howling went on for hours, along with the frantic sounds of battle and mayhem. Bodies slammed against the door, and for once, she didn't curse the thickness of the barrier, not when it was the only thing keeping her safe.

Over the next day, the chaos, or the noise of it anyway, subsided until only a chilling silence remained. A quiet that once she would have welcomed but now feared as hunger made her belly rumble. What had happened to her jailers? The vampire who brought her here? *Did they all leave?*

One day stretched into two then three, and she grew weak with only the water from the rusted sink to sustain her.

I'm going to die here.

Just not in the way she'd initially assumed. Before, she'd imagined Roderick or his minions killing her. Now . . . Now the joy she'd thought she'd feel at never seeing them again paled as the horror of dying by starvation hit her.

No. I can't die this way. Not without a fight or a chance, locked in a room with no way to escape. For the millionth time, she clung to the bars that covered the tiny window. The glass was long gone, and weeds provided a curtain across the opening.

She screamed until she was hoarse. "Someone. Help me. Please!"

For hours she called, delirious with hunger, her body weakening. A presence pulsed in her head, a wild thing that howled as her mind shattered and she forgot who she was. But she still retained enough to know freedom lurked just past the portal. She could smell it. Craved it. Pined for it. A death grip on the bars, she slept standing up, her forehead on the wall, not caring that the rough cinderblocks scraped her skin.

The tingle in her fingers woke her, and she peered up to see them bathed in a sprinkle of moonlight. The odd sensation prickled then burned, and before her horrified gaze, hair sprouted on the backs of her hands.

An agonized scream made its way out, even with her abused vocal cords. Pain. *Oh my God, the pain.* She dropped to her knees then hit the floor on her side, body thrashing. Awareness retreated as she hid in her mind in the little room she'd built for herself for when Roderick visited. She hid in her safe spot and left her dying body alone.

When the door to the cell opened, she never even noticed, but the wolf in her prison did, and it lunged for freedom.

Next book in the series: New Pack Order

www.ingramcontent.com/pod-product-compliance
Lightning Source LLC
LaVergne TN
LVHW012034070526
838202LV00056B/5499